TOO CLOSE TO HOME

"Wait a second, kid."

I look up. His eyes search my face, and I fight the urge to glance away.

He says, "What's your name?"

"Robert Frost." The lie comes easy. I hope he won't ask me for ID, but I hope my face shows I have it. "Like the poet."

He doesn't ask. "Sorry. Thought I knew you from . . . somewhere."

I shrug. Then, with a hint of a southern accent no Miamian would recognize as fake, I say, "You have some chocolate on your badge."

"Thanks." He goes to wipe it, and I start to walk away.

His voice stops me.

"Kinda young, aren't you?"

"Nineteen."

"Runaway?"

"No, sir. Wanted to see the world. Took off after senior year and been to twenty-eight cities since then."

I shouldn't have come back to Miami.

Also by Alex Flinn

BREATHING UNDERWATER
BREAKING POINT
FADE TO BLACK

NOTHING
TO
LOSE

Alex Flinn

HarperTempest
An Imprint of HarperCollins*Publishers*

Library of Congress Cataloging-in-Publication
Data
Flinn, Alex.
    Nothing to lose / by Alex Flinn.—1st ed.
        p.   cm.
    Summary: A year after running away with a
traveling carnival to escape his unbearable home
life, sixteen-year-old Michael returns to Miami,
Florida, to find that his mother is going on trial
for the murder of his abusive stepfather.
    ISBN 0-06-051750-6
    ISBN 0-06-051751-4 (lib. bdg.)
    ISBN 0-06-051752-2 (pbk.)
    [1. Runaways—Fiction. 2. Wife abuse—
Fiction. 3. Murder—Fiction. 4. Mothers and
sons—Fiction. 5. Trials (Murder)—Fiction.
6. Miami (Fla.)—Fiction.] I. Title.
PZ7.F6395No 2004   2003013959
[Fic]—dc22

Typography by R. Hult
❖
First paperback edition, 2005
www.harpertempest.com

For my mother and grandmother

ACKNOWLEDGMENTS

The author would like to thank the following people for their contributions to this book:

My readers, Marjetta Geerling and Laurie Friedman, as well as my critique group; my agent, George Nicholson, and his invaluable assistant, Paul Rodeen, for wonderful advice; Assistant State Attorney Mary Cagle, and Mary Mastin, RN, for research help; Joyce Sweeney, reader, handholder, and friend; my husband, Gene, for technical and other support, and my children, Katie and Meredith, for all the times I said, "Mommy's trying to think," and they let me; my "amazing" editor, Antonia Markiet—whose faith helped me create the pieces of the puzzle and whose talents helped me put them together. Thank you again and again.

Jury Selection Begins In Monroe Murder Trial

Jury selection will begin in the case of a Miami woman accused of bludgeoning her husband to death last March.

Despite the intense publicity surrounding the case, Lisa Monroe's defense attorneys failed in attempts to have the trial transferred from Miami.

Monroe, 35, a former legal secretary, is charged with murdering her husband, prominent local attorney and philanthropist Walker James Monroe, last March. Monroe plans to claim a battered-spouse-syndrome defense at trial. Her son, Michael Daye, now 17, has been missing since shortly before the alleged homicide took place.

See: TRIAL, Page 9A
Also: BATTERED-SPOUSE-SYNDROME DEFENSE, 1B

THIS YEAR

I shouldn't have come back to Miami.

The cop at the Whack-a-Mole game is a fat one. He dips his elephant ear into its cup of chocolate sauce like a buzzard with a tasty slice of roadkill. When his attention's on that, I approach.

"Give it a try, Officer?"

I have to shout over the screams from the Tilt-a-Whirl. That makes it easier to keep my voice steady. I've been escaping cops' notice for a year now—since I ran away. Secret is, don't avoid them and act casual. I was always old-looking for my age. Now, with the beard I grew, you'd never guess I'm still a week from being seventeen. That, and the way my hair's bleached white by the sun, conceals my identity. I'm no longer Michael Daye, high school athlete with a promising future. Now I look like someone with *no* future. I look like a carny.

That's what the cop sees, standing there. A carny.

"Nah, I'm on duty." He goes back to the elephant ear.

"Some other time, then." I start toward the next mark.

"Hold on, kid!"

I turn. Another cop, a female one, has joined the elephant-ear cop.

"You know you want to play," she says to him.

I stand, looking down, but not too far down, until the big cop waves me off again. I walk away, but I'm alert to their conversation even as the Tilt-a-Whirl starts. In my situation you can't afford to let your guard down.

"Put the mole in the hole," I call to the marks. "We're looking for racers. We're looking for Whack-a-Mole chasers." Across from me at the basketball toss, a winning player tries to decide between posters of Elvis or Bart Simpson, Britney Spears or Jesus.

"You at the courthouse today?" the female officer asks the other one.

He laughs. "It's a freakin' sideshow. They don't got sideshows at the carnival anymore—just the court-house."

"That bad?"

I go to help a mother and son. I take in the woman's worn-down shoes and worn-out face and think of my own mother. She used to take me to the carnival too, Tuesdays like today, when they let you in cheap if you saved up bread wrappers. Mom and I always ate lots of toast the month the fair was in town.

I miss my mother. It's been almost a year since I saw her. I can pretend to forget about her most of the time, but not here. Not in Miami.

"Just one." The mom points to the kid.

I count out her change and lean down to the kid. "You know how to play, Champ?"

"*No problemo*. The moles come out of their holes, and you bash their brains in."

"Actually," I say, "it works better if you hit soft."

Behind me the cops are still talking.

"So, lot of reporters there?" the female says.

"You name it—Court TV, all the locals. I think there was even a station from Cuba."

"I don't get it. What's the big deal about this case?"

The fat cop snorts. "What you don't get is a lot. You been on the force as long as I have, you know which cases'll get the attention. This one's got it all: a violent murder, a rich guy, and a beautiful woman who's guilty as sin."

I feel myself flinch, knowing for sure now. The woman they're talking about is my mother.

"You think?" the female cop asks. "I'm not so sure."

"What's her defense?" the other cop says. "She brained him with a stinking fire poker."

"She's saying he beat her up."

"That's what they all say. If it was so bad, why didn't she leave the poor slob? That's what I want to know. Why didn't she leave?"

I wait for him to answer his own question. He does.

"She's a gold digger, that's why. She married the old

man for the cash. Then she got tired of hearing him snore, so she killed him."

I make myself walk over to the game controls. I stand there one minute, hand on the switch, listening as one by one the sounds around me evaporate, and I hear instead the ocean outside my bedroom window. The old helplessness washes over me like a wave. I hadn't stayed to protect her.

"Hey, kid!"

The cop's voice penetrates my head's silence.

"You! Game-op!"

I turn to face him. He's finished his elephant ear and is checking his uniform for stains. He looks up, and I think I see a flash of recognition in his eyes. Then it's gone.

"Yes, sir?"

"I'll take a chance." He reaches for his pocket, real slow, knowing what I'll say next.

I say it. "On the house, Officer." I lean to check his station. Each board has a balloon that fills with air as you bash the mechanical moles. First one to pop a balloon is the winner.

"Wait a second, kid."

I look up. His eyes search my face, and I fight the urge to glance away.

He says, "What's your name?"

"Robert Frost." The lie comes easy. I hope he won't

ask me for ID, but I hope my face shows I have it. "Like the poet."

He doesn't ask. "Sorry. Thought I knew you from . . . somewhere."

I shrug. Then, with a hint of a southern accent no Miamian would recognize as fake, I say, "You have some chocolate on your badge."

"Thanks." He goes to wipe it, and I start to walk away.

His voice stops me.

"Kinda young, aren't you?"

"Nineteen."

"Runaway?"

"No, sir." I smile and hitch my thumbs into my pockets. "Wanted to see the world. Took off after senior year and been to twenty-eight cities since then."

I shouldn't have come back to Miami.

"Where you from, Robert?"

"Lennox, Louisiana." *Loosiana.* A lie. "The sticks."

People are looking at us, and the cop's friend nudges him. "Hey, you're holding up the works."

The cop looks at her, then the crowd. Then at me.

"Sorry, kid. You go ahead."

"No problem."

I turn toward the game controls. I make myself move slow. Behind me I hear the cop say, "He just looked so familiar." I throw the switch, and all around me mechanical moles start popping up. Every station is filled, and they're whacking, whacking, filling my ears and my brain with the noise, obliterating every feeling but loneliness and every thought but one: *I shouldn't have come back to Miami.*

THIS YEAR

An hour later I find my friend Cricket working at the double Ferris wheel.

"I can't stay here," I say.

"Cops buggin' you?" Cricket gets harassed by cops all the time. He says he's twenty but looks younger. "What I do is I keep a copy of my birth certificate with me at all times. Just makes life easier."

He leans to get it under the switch for the ride—a crumpled, Xerox-copied sheet of gray paper that identifies him as Jason Dietz, born twenty years ago in Kansas.

"That's your real birth certificate, Jason?"

He shrugs.

"It's not just the age thing with me," I whisper. "I ran away. There could be people looking for me."

Cricket folds the paper back up. "No one looks for teenaged runaways. You're a low priority. We've got our own little foster-care system here at the carnival. They give you a bunk to sleep in and all the corn dogs you can handle. Long as you're not obvious about it, no one much cares."

He goes back to what he's doing. I head for my joint, though my break's not over. It's getting later. The crowds are getting heavier, which makes it easier to hide. But tonight, here, it's just more people who might know me. I feel lost in a sea of eyes. Cricket doesn't get it. Being underage and a runaway still isn't the whole story, a story I maybe need to stay and tell. I bump into a woman, and she glares at me. I duck my head and move on.

When I return, the cop from earlier is there again, playing. I hang back. I remember what he said: *Guilty as sin. Why didn't she leave the guy? A gold digger.*

They don't know the whole story.

LAST YEAR

From the outside, the house looked okay. That didn't always mean anything.

Tristan let out a low whistle. "I still can't believe you freakin' live here, Daye. You so lucked out."

"It's just a house," I said.

"My gramma's place in Little Gables, where she lets us crash on the couches where the cats don't sleep— that's a house. This is a mansion. A compound. An estate. A—"

"Look, it's a house, Tris." Tristan's muffler was bad, and I wanted to get inside before the truck's idling motor woke someone. "And it's two A.M."

"That's class. Bum rides off me, then don't even—"

"Thank you." I opened the door, then shut it as fast as I could without slamming. I forgot to wave good-bye until his pickup had sputtered into darkness. I turned the key, hearing the ocean behind the house.

It wasn't Tris's fault. We'd been tight since sixth grade, when my mother finally gave in and let me play football. We were lots alike—both our moms worked as paralegals, and we'd lived on the edge of a school district where everyone else had a trust fund. Neither of us had fathers—not even dads-on-weekends like most guys. Mine ditched when I was two. Tris said his could be "anyone at South Miami High the same year as my mom." Other guys' dads embarrassed themselves, screaming in joy or agony at our football games. Tris and I, we didn't have to worry about that.

But lately I only saw Tris at school and at practice. Tris thought it was because I'd moved to a better neighborhood and bailed on him. I never corrected that. I also never told him why I had to rush home after practice. Sometimes, when he said I was lucky, I wondered if he was really that clueless.

I didn't turn on the light inside. My eyes got used to the darkness.

As soon as they did, I'd look for the runner. That was what Mom called the piece of embroidered fabric on the hallway table. It was always the first thing I noticed when I came in. In my situation, you learned to look for signals.

Since Mom married Walker, she'd been working on her embroidery, day after day, week after week, trapped in the house like that queen in the fairy tale she used to read me—the queen who spun straw into gold. She'd done that runner about a year ago, and since then it had been draped there—a Christmas gift for Walker, but it was a frequent target on his pissed-off days too.

"I'll rip it," he'd threatened the week before. "Then I'll rip you."

But that night it was safe on the table. Check. Somehow, I knew if Walker ever really ripped that runner, it would mean trouble.

I took off my shoes and walked on careful feet. Through the living room, neat too. Neater than neat. When my mother wasn't embroidering, she cleaned like her life depended on whether there was dust in the corners of the gleaming tile floors. And maybe it did.

Dining room—check. Kitchen—check. Library, sitting room, study—all fine. Even the fireplace poker in the study was arranged at the perfect angle.

I began to breathe.

It was always there, when I was home, but especially when I wasn't. The thought: *What was happening? What was he doing to her?* When I was at school or at football practice or partying with my friends. Any time I started having fun, I wondered.

And I'd had fun that night, the first I'd had in a while. I deserved it. Tris had dragged me to this party at Alex Ramos's house, a senior party, but we got in because, rumor had it, we were going to make varsity next year. I even hooked up with Vanessa, a cheerleader whose double-Ds were a sort of goal line for every guy on the J.V. team. I'd scored a first down, removed her bra and almost her shirt, in the porch swing in Alex's yard. I could have gotten more yardage, but the whole time I was thinking: *What is Walker doing to her?*

I finished my inspection and crept up the dark stairs.

My door never creaked when it opened. I'd made sure of that. I stripped off my clothes and got into bed in the dark. I didn't even brush my teeth, though the smell of my breath—stale beer—grossed me out.

The night was quiet, quieter still after the lights and music of the party. And I was alone, more alone than even in the crowds at school. I lay thinking about Vanessa. She'd told me to call her. I'd agreed, though I knew I was lying, which made me a shit on top of everything else.

Then I realized I wasn't alone.

I felt the presence and braced myself. Cowered, really. Cowered like the coward I was, wondering what I'd done to wake Walker. Wondering what he'd do about it.

"Hi." It wasn't Walker.

"Mom . . . you'll wake him."

She sat on my bed and reached for the light switch. "He's not home. He had his dinner and went back to the office."

How had I missed that? The absence of Walker's black Mercedes was an obvious all-clear.

"When's he due back?"

Her glance darted toward the window, and she didn't answer. I noticed the way her long, white nightgown hung on her. When had she gotten so thin? But her skin was tanned, her hair streaked blond like the other rich lawyers' wives. She didn't hang with them or do whatever it was they did. Tennis, maybe. Or volunteer work. Not her. Her tan came from sitting on the balcony, sewing, waiting for Walker to come home.

Still, she looked good. She was young for a mom, and if you didn't know her, you'd think she was happy.

But I knew her.

"How was practice today?" she asked.

"Great. I'll probably make varsity next year."

"That's fantastic." But she looked distracted, like she hadn't heard me.

"I didn't save you dinner," she said. "I'm sorry."

"I didn't think you would."

"I would have, if I could, but—"

"You could have."

"Walker thinks if you miss dinner, you shouldn't get it saved."

"And what Walker says, goes."

"That's right. He's your father . . . as close to a father as you've had anyway, and—"

"That's not very close."

"Michael, please."

I looked away. Mom had made all kinds of promises about Walker. A real family, everything perfect like a television sitcom. Maybe he'd even adopt me. And, of course, hot and cold running money. The money was the only part that worked out. I'd known the rest was a lie anyway. Even when they were dating, she'd come home with bruised arms or start wearing a scarf around her neck in ninety-degree heat. And there were his phone calls at three in the morning. I remembered those, too.

"You should leave him," I said.

She laughed. "You think it's easy because you don't remember how it was, living paycheck to paycheck, never sure if we'd make rent."

I did remember. Once there was a paper on our door, signed by the sheriff, threatening to put us out on the street. A few days later she'd gotten the job as Walker's secretary. A week after that they'd had their first date.

"I remember we were safe," I said.

She winced, like *I* was the one hitting her. She buried her head in her hands, starting the same old guilt trip. Usually it would have worked, but something about that night kept me going, made me say, "He's doing it more and more."

"That's not true."

"You think I don't notice, but I do." I pulled up the sleeve of her robe, revealing a mottled collection of bruises on her arms, some new, some gone purple and gold. "I'm not stupid, you know."

She still didn't look at me. Everything was silent except the insistent sound of Biscayne Bay behind us.

Then, from the other side of the house, the garage door rumbling up. Walker's motor.

Mom snapped off the light. She stood.

"At least think about it," I said.

She walked toward the door. It wasn't until she got there that she finally spoke.

"Michael?" Barely a whisper.

"What?"

"He says he'll kill us both if I leave."

Downstairs the garage door rumbled down.

THIS YEAR

Back at my trailer, I fumble under the mattress for the photo. It used to be in my wallet, which is why I have it even though I left home in a hurry. When I'm lonely, I look at it.

Like now. It's one of those photo-booth pictures, maybe even from the fair. In the picture I'm about twelve, wearing this so-cool-you-want-to-smack-me expression, which, after a year with the carnival, I now know is universal to all twelve-year-old suckheads everywhere. Mom looks happy. We're pre-Walker.

I've looked at it so many times that now, when I think of my mother, I can only see how she looked in the photo. I wonder if she ever really existed. Maybe I wish she didn't.

I stare at it a second longer before shoving it under my mattress. Eleven other guys sleep in this trailer, and there's not much you can do to keep stuff from getting gone through.

I wish I had a photo of Kirstie, too. But it's okay. I remember her. Kirstie was a carny too, one I loved last year, maybe still love. She was the one who started me on the road I'm on now. If I can find her, maybe she'll help me figure out where I'm going.

LAST YEAR

Once in driver's ed we saw this movie about hydroplaning. That's when the road's wet and the water picks up your car and makes it skid. The movie said the reason hydroplaning causes accidents is people fight it. It's instinct to try not to skid.

But what you really need to do is the opposite. Accept it. You want to be safe, just keep your hands on the wheel and turn into the skid.

I was in a skid those weeks before I left—with Walker, my mom, my friends. And if I fought it, I'd crash and burn.

I fought it.

Monday, after I talked to Mom, I went to Coach Lowery's office to tell him I couldn't play football.

Coach reacted with the concern and compassion you'd expect from an educator.

"You're shittin' me, right? You gotta be shittin' me."

"I wouldn't . . . do that, Coach."

Coach's office was full of wrestling trophies and smelled like old sweat and the Clorox they used on the floor. He ran his hand through hair that wasn't there, then banged his fist on the desk.

"You waltz in here and say, 'I'm quitting, Coach.

Sorry.' Like it's nothing. Like the Dolphins are nothing."

"It's not nothing, Coach. It's—"

"Darn right! I was going to start you at QB this fall. Is that nothing?"

I gaped at him. Starting quarterback! And only going into junior year. Usually positions like that went to seniors, and the best I could've hoped for was backup. I'd been playing football since Pop Warner, bumming rides off people, even walking to practice, all for this—and for the chance of catching the eye of some recruiter and getting out of here once and for all.

Not to mention the game itself. Most guys I knew played because their dads pushed them or to get girls. But I never had a dad to push me like that. And girls— they started calling me back when I still only wanted to play G.I. Joes. No, it was the game, the feel and smell of the ball on my hands. The high—better than beer or even the X I'd tried at a party once—the high of being tackled by a bigger, faster player, but you'd already made the perfect pass.

Then I remembered why I couldn't play.

"I'm sorry, Coach. I am."

"You on drugs?"

"No, sir."

"Because your work in history's been for shit. I been

passing you through—since I know you're trying hard—but that can't go on forever."

Message, Loud and Clear: He'd flunk me in history if I quit. For a second my mind screamed, *Tell him! Tell him the truth!* But no. I'd already tried that once, telling a teacher. Mr. Zucker had reported it to the authorities as apparently required by state law. But when the social worker showed up, a tired-looking woman, Walker had explained it away, saying I was having a little trouble "adjusting." He thanked her for her interest and said he'd take care of it. After she left, he had. Mom hadn't come out of her room for two days.

"I'm sorry," I told Coach again.

"Wanna clue me in on what makes the best player I have decide to throw away his life? And ruin things for everyone else, too?"

"I can't."

I'd come home from a game. A game we'd won, so I should have been happy. But the whole time, I'd wondered why she wasn't there. She'd always gone to my games, if only to worry about my getting hurt. I didn't know I cared. But that night, I looked out into the stands and didn't see her. I fumbled a gift of a pass, thinking about it, so everyone gave me shit the rest of the half.

When I got home, I knew it was happening.

I stood there, my feet feeling stapled to the floor. And

then the grip was released, and I was running, shoving past doorways and stairs like they were defensive linemen I should have gone through, hearing her screams, flying, falling across the dark, slick, wooden floor to Walker's study.

The room was bright with moonlight. From the door, I could see Walker's back, her blond hair. I stepped closer. His hands gripped her neck.

"Will you make me?" he screamed. "Will you make me do it again, you bitch?"

I started toward them.

"No. No don't." Her eyes met mine. "Michael, don't."

At my name, Walker turned and saw me. Then I was over him, on him, hands on his throat. On top of him, screaming, "You bastard! Get off of her!" feeling him struggle beneath me. All the strength that had been sapped in football flowed back through me, letting me hold him down, letting her get away.

Except she didn't get away. She stood there, like she didn't know whom to protect.

Walker rolled on top of me, but instead of hitting back, he just slipped away. He stared, the anger in his face evaporating.

He stood and walked out.

That's when she moved.

"Oh, baby," she said. "Oh, Michael, I'm sorry."

She tried to hug me, but I pulled away. I kept her away. Her shirt was ripped at the neck. There were bruises shaped like his hands. I felt nothing looking at her. Or maybe I hated her.

"It won't happen again," she said. "I promise."

I was so sure she would leave. Or, even if she didn't, everything would change. I was strong now. He knew I'd take him on. He wouldn't do it again, not now.

But the next week, another game missed. And when I got home, this eerie déjà vu. My footsteps followed the same path to the same room, same place. But this time Walker fought back. I missed the next three days of school because of the pain. Walker's arm was in a sling too. I didn't confront him after that. Didn't, because I knew if I did, someone would get killed.

So instead, I watched. There was nothing else I could do. I was too weak.

"I just can't play, Coach."

I placed my locker key on his desk. I felt his eyes follow me out the door and down the hall. I didn't let myself look back.

•   •   •

By lunch, I still hadn't told Tristan.

"Let's roll," he said as we left fourth-period Spanish. Coach was posting scrimmage teams today, and though he wouldn't post the real roster until fall, we'd figured these teams would give us an idea of his plans. Tris had packed up his stuff five minutes before the bell rang. "You go," I said. "Tell me what it says."

"Yeah, right." He laughed. "It'll be so cool if we both make varsity next year."

I followed him downstairs and across the breezeway, trying to find my nerve. When we got to the P.E. office, lots of guys were already there. My friends were high-fiving and slapping backs. Tristan started pushing through to look.

"Wait," I said.

He stopped, looking at me like, *Well?*

"I quit the team, Tris."

"Yeah, right. What'd you, go out for track instead?" He started back toward the door.

I grabbed his shoulder. "Listen to me. I quit for real, okay? It's a dumb game. I don't have time for it. I'm practically flunking history, and my mom is on me about it. Okay?"

I realized I was shouting. I elbowed past Tris and some other guys to get down the hall.

Tristan followed me. "For real, even? Your mom was so into you playing. Is it your stepdad?"

"Just leave me alone!"

I felt his eyes on me as I left, expecting something. Seemed like someone—Coach, Tristan, Mom—was always expecting something from me. I headed to the cafeteria, figuring I'd be safe from questions there. Most of my friends got lunch from the "roach coach," this truck that parked behind the basketball courts and sold stuff like greaseburgers with a side of grease.

But Vanessa was in the cafeteria with half the cheerleading squad. I hadn't called her over the weekend. When the cheerleaders saw me, they started to giggle and talk faster. I gave myself a pep talk about how dumb cheerleading really was, and I kept eating my lunch—pb&j's from home. A minute later Vanessa strolled past my table to put her tray onto the conveyor belt.

"Hi," I said.

She lowered her eyes, cool. Her look said she wasn't going to sit by me without an engraved invitation. Lots of girls would've been on my lap. That was what was so cool about Vanessa. Well, that and her breasts. But I didn't invite her, and she went back to her friends.

I didn't really like her. That's what I told myself. She was pretty and all, but not a whole lot better or worse than any other girl. I finished my first pb&j and opened the second, not looking up. But then I sensed someone sitting beside me. And, more than that, watching me.

I'd known Julian Karpe since kindergarten, one of those weird grade-school friendships that starts over a shared Tonka truck and keeps going long after you've grown past it. When we got to middle school, I went out for football, and that was pretty much that. I tried to talk Karpe into playing, but he said it was stupid. He blew me off after that. I made some new friends and forgot about Karpe.

So it was weird, him sitting by me. I watched him a minute, sort of marveling at his white skin, which looked like it had never seen the sun—tough on Key Biscayne. He read a book, oblivious to the decibel level in the cafeteria, and when he noticed me looking at him, he lifted two spidery fingers to his brow in a salute.

"Hey, Mikey Mouse!" Karpe and I used to make up stupid nicknames for everyone . . . back when we were seven.

"Hey." Hoping answering would stop him repeating my name. Was Vanessa looking?

"She's really all that and a bag of Doritos, huh?" He nodded toward Vanessa.

"Hadn't noticed. See ya." I got up and left.

My locker was by the gym, same as all my friends' lockers. Usually we hung there, but now I wanted to get my junk and leave before they all got on my case.

I'd done the right thing, I knew. It just felt so damn wrong.

THIS YEAR

The Internet White Pages prompts:

Last Name:

I type: *Anderson*

First Name: Kirsten

I leave the city and state blank. I have no idea where Kirstie is.

The message comes back red.

State

I choose Louisiana, where she said she was from.

No matches found.

Good thing about working for the carnival is that carnies sleep during the day. For insomniacs like me, that means I have a lot of time on my hands. Today I took two buses and a train to the downtown library, where they have out-of-town phone books. I'm trying the Internet first, though.

I type in different combinations:

Andersen, Kirsten

Andersen, Kirstie

Anderson, Kersten

Anderson, K

Twenty-one matches for *K. Anderson* in Louisiana. I print them out, then try Florida, where I last saw her, then Georgia and Alabama, because I don't really know if she went home. I avoid thinking about the obvious . . . that she's changed her name, is unlisted, is living with family.

Is living with another guy.

That Kirsten Anderson wasn't her real name in the first place.

That she's dead.

There are five Kirsten Andersons in Minnesota, but Minnesota isn't a likely state. Too cold. When I picture Kirstie, it's always hot. She wears a green T-shirt and short denim shorts, her dark hair flowing out behind her, nothing you'd wear in Minnesota.

I print the Minnesota list anyway.

I don't know why I need to find Kirstie. I mean, I *do* know, because I love her, but finding her won't solve my problems. It might make more.

Still, I try Arkansas, New York, California.

"You need to move on."

I start. Instinctively I pull my baseball cap lower on my forehead. "What?"

"Your time's up. It's someone else's turn at the computer now."

I look sideways. It's a library employee.

"Oh, sorry," I say. "Can I use it again later?"

She sighs. "I'll put you back on the list."

"Where are the out-of-state phone books and the newspaper microfilms?"

She leads me toward the telephone books. I find Louisiana and select the one that includes Kirstie's town. There are a bunch of Andersons, but only one in her town, a woman's name. Not likely to be her. Still, I copy the number. Maybe it's an aunt or something. I copy the other Andersons in nearby towns.

I start toward the newspaper archives, then go for the current paper instead. The headline reads:

Jury Selection Difficult in Highly Publicized Monroe Case
Trial may begin next week

There's a photograph of a guy, maybe Mom's lawyer, and one of Mom and Walker, taken at some party she and Walker went to once. I stare at it. Other than my one photo, I haven't seen her face in a year. I wonder if she's changed as much as I have.

"Robert Frost?"

I look up.

"It's your turn for the computer again." The woman smiles. "And I love your name."

"Thanks. My mom was into poetry."

She glances at what I'm reading, then at my face. I'm

sure she knows who I am. I'm him. I'm the kid. I can't make my hands pull down my baseball cap, and even if I could, it wouldn't matter.

"Fascinating case," she says. "Isn't it?"

"Oh, yeah."

"Do you think she's guilty?"

I fold the newspaper and put it back onto the rack. "You know, I found what I need after all. You can let someone else take my turn."

I wait until her back is turned before I walk out.

LAST YEAR

The dining room at Walker's house (I never called it *our* house) overlooked Biscayne Bay. It was only a few feet from the study where, according to today's *Miami Herald* (though they used the word *allegedly*), Walker would soon lie, murdered by his gold-digging wife. But that day Walker was in perfect health. He sat in his armchair, holding a glass of Jack in one hand, a cancer stick in the other, waiting for my mother to get dinner on the table.

I sat with him. "Those things will kill you, Walk," I said.

"You'd like that, wouldn't you?" Walker checked his watch, and I checked mine. Six fifty-eight. Mom always had dinner on the table at seven—no earlier, and definitely no later.

I laughed. "Just concerned for your health's all. They say lung cancer's a slow, painful way to go."

"Don't worry, kid. I'm going to live forever."

"I know it, Walk. You're too mean to die."

I laughed again—just kidding. The house rule was pleasant dinner conversation. This was what passed for it. I was counting the nanoseconds until I could go back to my room, cram for a history test I now needed to ace. Walker made me eat with them. I knew I shouldn't bait him like I did, like poking an alligator with a stick. But I hated it, hated sitting there every night, pretending things were beautiful. I hated myself for pretending too.

"Remember that," Walker said.

"Almost ready!" my mother called from the kitchen.

Walker exhaled smoke in my face. "No hurry, hon. Better to do it right than do it quick." He glanced at his watch. Six fifty-nine. "It smells wonderful."

"I'll help you," I said to her.

"I'm fine." That came from the kitchen. "You two talk."

Talk. I knew I was going to have to tell them about football. Otherwise there'd be questions about missed practices. And besides, I wanted to tell them, wanted to let Walker know I'd be around, whatever good that would do. So I sat in silence, planning to spit out the information over dessert, then bail to my room. That was my plan, anyway.

Within the minute, my mother had the feast on the table. Tonight it was lamb, the kind with little paper booties on its feet. Blood pooled beside it on the plate. She scooped roast potatoes on top, and the bloody mess disappeared.

"Looks great, Mom." I missed the days when we'd lived on spaghetti and peanut butter.

"Thanks." She glanced at Walker. We both did. He

sawed his meat, then chewed the first bite. Would it be too tough? Underdone? I cut a potato with my fork, then held one half aloft. I wasn't watching Walker. I wasn't waiting for him.

Finally, he spoke.

"Good stuff, Lisa. I always tell people I got the prettiest gal and the best cook, too."

"No, you don't. That would be too embarrassing."

"I sure do," he insisted. "Everyone wishes they were me." He reached for her ass, and she sort of screamed, but laughed, too.

I grimaced. No one noticed. When Walker finished groping her, Mom started in with the whole *Leave It to Beaver* family routine.

"Anything interesting happen at school, Michael?"

I started to tell her about quitting the team, then stopped. There was time.

"We're reading *The Great Gatsby* in English."

Mom smiled. "I loved that book in high school. It's a great love story."

"You think?" I said. "I thought . . . wasn't the guy sort of . . . obsessed? I mean, it's been a while since I read it."

"You said you were reading it now," Walker said.

"I already read it. I did a report on it in eighth grade."

"You should read it again," Walker said. "A good student would read it again. That's your problem—always taking the easy way out."

"I am a good student," I said, pushing back thoughts of history. I'd *been* a good student before Walker. But Mom was giving me a look, so I added, "I planned to read it again."

Walker nodded, and I stuffed the potato into my mouth. Mom turned to Walker.

"And how was your day?"

Which was enough to set the Walk-man off on his favorite topic.

"I am a victim of affirmative action," he said. "What does it take for a non-Latin, white male to get ahead in this town?"

I'm sure you're going to tell us. I tried to get the paper off the lamb chop.

"What happened?" Mom asked.

"Lost my motion. Damn Judge *Hernandez*, of course, finds for the plaintiff, who is—of course— another bean eater, represented by a third bean eater."

I twisted the paper, first one way, then the next, remembering some kiddie show I saw once with a lamb named *Lamb Chop*. Did Lamb Chop end up as lamb chops? I almost laughed.

"It can't be that bad," my mother told Walker.

"You don't know anything about it," Walker snapped.

Mom crossed her arms to her chest. "I just meant . . ."

"Who cares what you meant? Just shut up."

We ate in silence a minute. Or at least Walker and Mom ate. I stared at my food.

Then Mom tried again. She spoke slowly, like she wasn't sure if he'd get mad.

"I just meant you're a wonderful lawyer. I've worked for lots, so I know. Your clients know—didn't Ray Cobo just bring all his product liability work to you?" She glanced up, not speaking, until Walker nodded. "And the judges respect you. You know you win a lot more than you lose."

"Of course I do." Walker laughed, relaxing. "I always win. We wouldn't live here if I didn't." He leaned toward her. "I wouldn't have you if I didn't."

"You'd always have me."

"Oh, of course. Pretty girl like you with an old geezer like me—if I lost my practice, you'd be out of here so quick the door wouldn't have time to slam."

"You aren't losing your practice." Confident now, she stroked his arm, playing with the hairs, leaning close to speak into his ear. "I'd love you even if you didn't have a cent."

Walker shook his head, but he turned to kiss her, his fat, hairy hand reaching out.

That's when he met my eyes.

"What are you doing?"

I jumped. I looked down. My hands were still working on the lamb chop paper. I'd managed to remove it. Then I'd shredded it, scattered the pieces across the floor. I didn't even remember doing it. I thought I was being careful, trying not to set him off like Mom always said. But I couldn't stand watching her suck up to him, and it was like the anger and fear inside me were living creatures that made my hands move by themselves.

Then they made me speak. "It looked dumb."

I actually *saw* a vein jump in Walker's neck. One hand still held Mom's. With the other, he clutched his fork.

"Clean it up." He banged the fork on the table.

"I'll do it," Mom said.

"No, you won't. He made the mess. He should clean it. It's the only way he'll learn."

I sat there, feeling my fingers still shredding the paper, making the last tiny piece into two. Four. *Stop it!*

"You little shit!" Walker rose from his seat.

I picked up a few pieces of paper, and Walker settled back down.

"That's better."

I ripped a piece in half.

Walker stood again. I flinched, but in a way, I wanted him to hit me so I wouldn't have to watch it anymore, so I could be the one hurting. The room was dead silent except for breathing and the sound of paper being ripped. I kept shredding the paper. I stared at him, daring him.

"Michael!" My mother looked first at me, then Walker. "It's okay. I'll get it." She knelt on the floor and started picking up the paper. I just kept shredding, smaller and smaller.

"Who in the hell asked you to do anything?" Walker threw down his fork. He stood, yanking her up by the arm, and I saw his fist clench. She winced.

"I just thought . . ."

"You just thought. You're so damn stupid. I tell you what to think." He shoved her to the floor. Then he looked at me, the anger cool in his eyes. "Quit it, I said."

Quit. I quit.

"Hey, you know . . . I quit the football team today."

Silence. I knew it would get a reaction, and it did. Walker stopped, maybe because I'd stopped shredding the paper, and Mom stared at me, getting up from the floor.

"What?" she said.

"I . . . quit . . . the . . . team." I said it slow. I'd thought about saying I'd gotten cut, but when it came down to it, I couldn't. I couldn't give Walker the satisfaction of thinking I wasn't good enough, and more, I couldn't let her get off thinking it wasn't her fault. I wanted her to know it was. I'd given up football because of her, her weakness. I wanted her to know I was staying home to take care of her when it should have been the other way around.

"Quit?" The paper petals fell from Mom's fingers and floated down. "But I thought—"

"I have other things to do now, more important things. Football's for kids. I don't have time for kids' stuff anymore, do I?"

Mom looked from Walker to me. "Oh, Michael, I'm so sorry. I know you loved it."

"What do you have to be sorry for?" Walker demanded. "Little wuss went and quit because that's just the kind of little wuss he is."

"I quit because I need to take care of other stuff."

"Michael, please . . ." My mother shifted in her seat.

"Wuss. Pansy." Walker stalked back to his seat and started cutting meat off the bone. "What's the matter? Didn't want to hurt your pretty face, Pretty Boy?"

"What would you know about it?"

"I played football in school, faggot."

"They let fat, bald guys play when you were in school?"

That stopped him a second, and it made me happy. Seeing the wiped-off smile on Walker's face made me want to shout in the street.

My mother picked up the vegetable bowl—broccoli,

cauliflower, and carrots mixed together—not the canned mixed veggies she used to buy, but fresh ones she made in a special bamboo steamer. She offered it first to Walker. "Well, I'm sorry to hear—"

"You're always sorry!" Walker shoved her away, hard. She stumbled, and the bowl shattered on the marble floor. He raised his arm. "Clumsy bitch. Clean it up!"

Tears of humiliation filled her eyes. Still, I knew better than to try and help. She went for the broom, and I just watched. I could tell by the way she moved that he'd hurt her. I was trembling by then, sitting in my seat watching the blood pooled on my plate.

"Eat your dinner," he demanded.

So much blood. Just looking at it, I felt my insides come up. "I can't," I said through my teeth.

"You will."

"I'm not going to. Maybe you can get her to do what you want, but not me. Not me."

I tried to keep my voice from shaking, but I could tell he heard it.

Still, I said, "Not me."

"Then there are going to be problems, because when I fight, I always win."

My mother came back then, broom and dustpan in one hand, a bottle of Fantastik in the other. "It'll just be a second."

Walker smiled and patted the seat beside him. "You know what? It can wait until after." He put his hand on her butt and guided her toward the seat. "I'd rather we all eat together as a family."

I pushed my bloody plate away. "You eat. I'm not hungry."

He watched me leave, not saying anything.

• • •

Fifteen minutes later Mom knocked on my door. "It's key lime pie."

"No way."

"Please, Michael. You know—"

"There is no way," I said, "no way in hell I'm eating pie with him. You want to pretend, you just go ahead."

"Please. Walker's trying, Michael. He really wants to be a family. We all just need to try a little harder."

"You try. Let me know when you're finished."

"You have no idea how hard this is."

She kept talking, but I'd stopped listening. Maybe I had it all wrong. Maybe his abuse of her wasn't a problem. Maybe she even liked it. Maybe she wasn't drowning, looking to me for rescue. Maybe instead, she was like a scuba diver, used to navigating rough waters, enjoying her swim with sharks.

THIS YEAR

The guy by the Whack-a-Mole wears a blue Florida Gators sweatshirt, but he's too young for college. He's my age. It's Julian Karpe.

"This is a cool game," he says to some guy. "Someone told me the secret once."

I feel a sucking feeling in my stomach's pit. I know who told him, and I know when. I walk to the side of the game by the hanging Barneys and Blue's Clues dogs. Part of me hopes they'll hide my face. The other part wants to go over to Julian, to say hi. *Hi, it's me.*

But maybe it's not Karpe at all. Sure, this guy sounds like Karpe, looks like him a little. But he's taller now, more filled out, and less of a geek. I put my hand to my own face. How have I changed in a year?

"Michael." Not a question. It's Karpe. I remove my hand from my face and stare at him.

He looks back, suddenly unsure. "It's you—right, Mike?"

No hablo inglés.

"Yeah. Yeah, it's me."

Karpe starts to clap me on the shoulder, then stops. "I wondered if you'd be here."

I say nothing.

"After what happened, after you . . . disappeared, the

police came around school. They asked if I knew where you were, but I said I hadn't seen you in close to a week. No one had."

"Are you going to play?" I ask.

"I wasn't sure where you went anyway. I suspected, but I never knew for sure until now."

I look to see if anyone's listening, but it's barely three on a Monday, and you could bowl on the sidewalks without hitting anyone. Karpe's finished talking, so I say, "Thanks," because I know he expects it. Because he deserves it, even.

"No problem. I figured you'd done nothing wrong. If you wanted to leave, you had your reasons."

I say, "If you're not going to play—"

"My stepmother's a lawyer, you know."

I manage a laugh. "Yeah? Well, my stepfather was a lawyer too. So what?"

"No, I mean . . . I mean maybe she could help you. Angela—that's her name—she does pro bono stuff sometimes. That means helping people for free, people who need help."

"Why would I need a lawyer?" But I know.

Karpe keeps going. "And she says there's this thing called attorney-client privilege. If you told her anything, I mean, about your mother, she'd have to keep it secret."

He takes something out of his pocket, which turns

out to be a business card. I know somehow he came here just to bring it. I also know I won't call his step-mother.

He says, "What I mean is, maybe she could tell you if there's something you could do to help your mother. Do you ever worry about your mother, Mike?"

"Don't call me that!" I glance around.

But he hands me the card. I look at it. "Thanks."

"Think about it."

He walks away. The sun's starting to sink, and the fair lights begin to rise—neon pink, yellow, and green, clashing with Karpe's electric blue and orange sweat-shirt. I'm alone again, listening to that old song that always brings the past back, brings Kirstie and my mom too close, too real. Karpe looks back at me, and I wave, showing the business card. When he turns away, I start to crumple it. Then I change my mind and shove it into my pocket instead.

• • •

That night there's a fight outside my trailer. Normally I wouldn't notice. There's always something going on outside, always someone awake so you never have to be alone. But tonight I turned in early. I plan on going to the library again tomorrow. I've run through all the K. Andersons I pulled the first time. I need to try some more states.

And something else. I'm thinking about what Karpe said about helping my mother. I let his words wash over me during the day, but now, lying in bed, not really tired enough to sleep, the thought keeps coming back to me. *Help her. Help her.* Playing in my head like a CD with a scratch on it, where it just keeps going back and playing the same part over and over.

Outside, people are bumping against the trailer walls, yelling. Finally I go out in T-shirt and boxers. There are four guys, including this one, Victor, who always reminds me of Walker Monroe.

I say, "Can you maybe move over there, guys? I have to get up early."

The others start to go along. They like me okay. But Victor swaggers to the door, kicking dropped beer bottles. He's shorter than me, but solid, and he likes to throw his weight around. Usually I avoid him.

"Need your beauty sleep, huh?" He turns to his friends. "Hey, Birdman here thinks this is the Plaza Hotel."

The guys laugh, drunk. Everyone calls me Birdman because the first week after I left home, I found this baby crow at a fairground in North Carolina. It had fallen from a tree, an ugly thing with hardly any feathers. It reminded me of the little bird in the book *Are You My Mother?*, which Mom used to read me (but when I said that, no one knew what I meant; none of the other carnies had mothers who read to them). I took it back to the trailer and tried to feed it bugs and stuff. Someone heard it chirping and told everyone. They all ragged on me. The bird had died anyway.

The story and the name stuck—made me sound like a wuss. But new guys thought the name had something to do with the Birdman of Alcatraz, so that made me scary. It was good having an identity anyway. It made me part of things in this place where no one has a past or much of a future.

Now, I say, "I don't think it's the Plaza, Vic. I'm just trying to sleep. Thought maybe you could just take it over there, that's all. Be decent."

Victor gets closer, moving to stand on the trailer steps so he's in my face. I smell booze—not just beer like the other guys—and that reminds me of Walker too.

"Make me, Birdman. My mama didn't teach me no manners, so I guess it's up to you."

"Aw, quit it, Vic," one of the other guys, my friend Johnny, says.

Victor ignores him.

"How 'bout your mama, Bird Boy?"

"Don't talk about my mother." But Victor doesn't know. That's what I like about the fair. No one knows or wants to know. The only one who knew was Kirstie, and Kirstie isn't here.

"Did your mama teach you manners, Bird?"

"Quit it."

"Or did she teach you to fight?" He pushes my shoulder. "Wanna fight, pretty boy? Little boy? I'm ready."

I feel my fists clench involuntarily and I raise my arm. I can tell how it would feel, hitting him. Satisfying for a second, fists crashing into his face, not just once, but again and again, hitting him until there's no hitting left.

I back away.

"Just . . . go over there. Would you, please?"

I go to close the door. Victor begins to follow me, but something—the look on my face, maybe—stops him.

"Faggot," he says.

I shut the door.

They stay into the night, their own fight over, concentrating instead on keeping me awake by pounding the trailer. I pull my pillow over my head, but in my mind, I see the photograph of my mother.

I don't go out again. Eventually the others come in to sleep. When my alarm goes off at five thirty, I let it ring long enough to wake everyone.

LAST YEAR

After one day in the school cafeteria, I went back to eating by the roach coach with my former teammates.

Tedder Dutton, a junior jock I didn't like much, was doing an impression of Miss Hamasaki, our English teacher. Lest the term *impression* leave anyone thinking of *Saturday Night Live* or *Mad TV*, I'll clarify. This impression consisted entirely of Tedder reading a poem from our English book in this phony accent, pulling his eyes back like a six-year-old pretending to be Asian.

"The roods are rovery, dalk and deep," he recited.

His friends laughed, and Tris said, "You have to wag your butt when you do it."

"She doesn't talk like that," I said. Then, to Tris, I added, "This is what happens when siblings mate."

"Hey, Daye, why do you always bring your lunch?" Tedder demanded. "The smell of peanut butter makes me want to regurgitate."

The two players laughed some more. I shrugged. "Healthier, I guess. I could complain that I'm sick of the sound your arteries make when they harden—but I'm too nice."

"Right," he said. "Gotta keep healthy for foot— . . . why *do* you have to keep healthy, Daye?"

I told him to bite me. Dutton was the type of guy

who'd let you do his sister if he could think of some way that it would improve his stats ("And if you haven't *seen* his sister," Tris had said). He'd get my position now that I was out. By my definition he should've been kissing my ass for allowing him to replace me. But Dutton saw it differently.

"Can't believe you ditched the Dolphins like that," he said.

"You did great in practice yesterday, Tedder," Tristan cut in. "Though you could pass to me a few times, instead of grabbing all the glory."

"Yeah, right," Tedder said. "You get glory when you earn it, second string."

Glory. There was this scrimmage last year, J.V. versus varsity. It had been third and fifteen, and J.V. was at the forty. The defense bore down on me, and I'd thrown this near-impossible pass to Tris. I could still feel my arm on the follow-through, and Deion Jacobs landing on me. I could hear our side cheering when Tris caught it and ran it in for a TD.

"Remember that scrimmage last year, Tris?" I said. "I passed to you."

Tris grinned. "Yeah, that was cool."

"But that was last year," Dutton said. "This year, we have a way better D. You guys would've taken the

L-train against this year's team."

"Don't know about that," Tris said. "Jackson got, like, huge over Christmas break. He juicin'?"

"Stephawn Jackson on 'roids?" Dutton looked shocked. "Nah, I think he gained twenty pounds— mostly in his forehead—by doubling up on his Flintstone vitamins."

Tristan laughed. "Hey, Mike, you going to Lucas's party Saturday?"

I looked from them to my sandwich. I wanted to go. Vanessa would be there. But the knowledge of what could happen at home if I went—it was always there like an old song that sticks in your head, where you can't stop hearing it no matter how hard you try.

Tris was looking back at me.

You don't know them anymore. You don't even know yourself.

Finally I said, "Wasn't invited."

"You don't need an invite." Tris slapped my shoulder. "We're all going."

"Yeah, I'm taking Vanessa DeLeon," Tedder said. "Looking forward to it too. I hear she has a weakness for men in uniform. What a hose monster."

The veins in my right arm tensed. It was a normal thing that, true or not, guys said about girls. On a normal day, I might have heard this with a nod, or at most called the guy an asshole. But that day I was ready to get majorly pissed at anyone who even minorly deserved it.

"What'd you say?" My voice was quiet.

"I said she's a sure thing." Tedder mimed hitting a home run.

"Take it back."

"What?"

I grabbed him by the collar. "Take it back, now." I felt my fist, the one that wasn't on his collar, clench. My pulse was racing, my arm was raised, and every molecule of my being was standing on end, knowing how good it would feel to hit him. Like soda bursting from a shaken bottle. Maybe this was how it felt to lose it—a relief.

"Hey, what are you crazy, man?"

The voice was Tristan's. It sounded like he'd said it more than once. And I felt the arms of one of the varsity players pulling me off Tedder, holding me back, then pushing me away. The guys were all around me, on me until I felt trapped. I couldn't breathe.

I pushed through them and stared at Tedder's red face. My fist unclenched, and I stood there, feeling it tingle a moment, barely knowing who or where I was. I'd never been a guy who started fights before. Who was I becoming?

I walked away.

Tedder's voice called after me, "You're lucky I'm in training, Daye. Otherwise, I'd have kicked your ass!"

No one followed me.

THIS YEAR

At the library later that morning, the headline of today's
Herald reads:

Life Sentence Likely If Monroe Convicted

I reach into my jeans pocket. The business card
Karpe gave me is still in there, and I touch it. Maybe I'll
go see his stepmother after all. Maybe there's a reason
he came to see me, even a reason I'm back in Miami at
all. I'd wanted to go with the fair to escape. But I can't
escape who I was, or what I still am.

LAST YEAR

That afternoon I got home early. As usual Mom was sewing on the balcony.

"I have an idea," I told her.

She jumped. "Oh, Michael. You scared me."

"Sorry. Hey, I thought we could take a run down on the beach."

I pointed to the sand below. Maybe if I could get her out of the house, I could, I don't know, talk to her. It was three thirty, hours still until Walker was expected home. She glanced at the sand, then at the portable phone beside her. "I don't know."

"Take the phone. It'll work down there. It's only a few feet. It's a beautiful day out."

She studied me, looking for an excuse to say no. It would be that—an excuse, not a reason. "Since when do teenaged boys want to run on the beach with their mothers? When I was your age, you couldn't get me away from my family fast enough."

"Well, I'm asking you." It was suddenly important to me to get her outside. "You used to want to run a marathon, remember? Now that you don't work, you could train for it."

She laughed. "That was a joke. I'm not strong

enough. It was fine saying that before when I could never . . . and Walker doesn't like female athletes anyway. He always says the other partners' wives spend too much time at the gym. He once told me he thought needlework was such an elegant thing to do."

I remembered him threatening to rip apart the runner she'd made.

"You should do what you're into, not just what Walker wants."

"I'm into this." She held up the fabric so I could see. The whole thing was covered in flowers with fancy, knotted centers that must have taken her days to stitch. "My grandmother taught me when I was little."

"But you hated it," I protested. "You said she trapped you in the house all summer and made you embroider tablecloths while your friends went to Girl Scout camp. You said you felt trapped." My mother was raised by her grandmother, and I remembered her telling me that she used to look out the window and wish she could go outside. Now she was doing the same thing. Or maybe she wasn't even *wishing* anymore.

"But Grandma Mavis was right. She said I was learning a valuable skill. The girls who went to camp—what did they learn, except to cook over a fire?"

"Might have come in handy a few times when the electricity got turned off."

"Well, we don't have to worry about that anymore." She started to stitch again. "I miss Grandma Mavis."

Which just proved how sucky things had gotten.

"I never met her, did I?" I asked.

She shook her head. "She never forgave me for getting married right out of high school. 'Just like your mother,' she said, 'a big disappointment.' She wanted me to go to college to study nursing. I was always best in my class in science. Did I ever tell you that about me?" The wind caught the fabric she was sewing, and she gathered it between her knees. "I wrote her when you were born, but she didn't come. When your father left, that's when she wrote back. She said I could stay with her if I gave you up for adoption. You were two." Mom shook her head. "Crazy old witch."

"Thought you missed her."

"Oh, I do. She just didn't understand." She looked at me. "You were such a sweet baby." She stopped stitching and stroked the fabric, which I now saw was some sort of coverlet for a crib. "I miss those times."

A horrible thought hit me. "You wouldn't have another baby, would you?"

I held my breath, waiting for an answer, picturing her stomach growing round and wide and having someone else to worry about. God, I was sick of worrying. I wanted to be like I used to. I wanted to play football and be selfish and make out with girls at parties, like Tedder and all those other guys I hated now, but used to like, could like again if I didn't have to hate them.

"No," she said. "Walker says no."

For once I agreed with Walker. But I said, "You could find someone else. You're only thirty-four."

She laughed. "Oh, that's what I'll do. I'll find someone else." She went back to the flower she was stitching. "What a thing to say. Walker's my husband."

"Your husband who threatened to kill you."

"I shouldn't have told you that. I was just upset that night."

"He still said it. I want to talk about it. I want to—"

She put her head down, hands to her ears. "I did this for you, Michael. You needed stability."

The words stung. There'd been a night in eighth grade. Tristan and I and these older guys had been spray painting a fence near school. Of course when the cops showed up, the older guys had scattered, and just Tris and I got caught. It was kids' stuff, but Mom had cried and said, "I don't know what to do with you. I wish you had a father to help with this."

She'd started seeing Walker soon after. But I wouldn't let her pin this on me.

"Let's go outside," I said. "I saw a dolphin the other day."

"Walker's working on his temper. We both have to help him, not do things to set him off." She put down the fabric and gazed at me. "He did a good job yesterday, when you got him so upset."

Huh? "He broke a bowl. He pushed you."

"It was just a bowl, though. And it was an accident." She finished the last petal of the flower and began another. How many hours had she spent on it today? I noticed that all the times we talked about why she stayed with Walker, she never said she loved him. She always made it about me, somehow.

"Let's go outside," I repeated.

She looked out again, for a long time this time, until I almost thought she would go.

"Please," I said.

"I want to finish this." She picked up the fabric again.

"He hurt you yesterday. I could tell."

"We have to be more understanding of Walker. He has a stressful job. That new secretary's incompetent, and his law partners don't appreciate—"

"He should beat up his partners then."

My mother laughed. "Sure. That's a good idea."

Then she didn't say anything, just kept sewing. The room was so still.

I said, "You know what the big problem is, with you being married to him?"

"Michael . . ."

I remembered grabbing Tedder, how good it would have felt to hit him. And how bad, too. And I thought, *Maybe the good part and the bad part are the same, like maybe if you do the dumbest, worst thing you can think of, there's nothing left to worry about.* I never would have thought that before. But now, it was like I was dying, but slowly. And all the good parts of me were dying first.

I said, "Before Walker, I used to think I was a nice guy. I might not have been the smartest guy or the richest or even the most athletic. But I was a nice guy."

"Of course you are. You're a sweet boy."

"No. No, I'm not. Because late at night, when I lie in bed, I wish he was dead."

She put down the needlework and looked at me a moment. "You don't really wish that."

"I do. What kind of person does that make me?"

THIS YEAR

Why are you here?

What are you doing?

You don't have to stay, you know. You can turn tail and leave down the service elevator, and no one will ever know.

I'll know.

The door to the lawyer's office is glass and dark wood. I reach for the handle, imagining the door shattering, splintering under my touch. But it doesn't, so I step onto the pink marble inside.

The receptionist gives me that special sneer adults reserve for teenagers in ripped jeans.

"May I help you?"

"I'm here to see Angela Guerra."

"Is *Ms.* Guerra expecting you?"

"I'm Michael." Intentionally leaving out my last name. "Her stepson, Julian, told me . . . he said I could come."

The woman presses a button on the intercom and speaks into it. She looks back.

"Have a seat. She'll be with you in a moment." I see her mentally add, *Don't touch anything.*

I do as I'm told. The lobby is big and too open. I sit and think about leaving. I don't know what I'm going to tell Angela Guerra, or even if I want to tell her anything at all.

Then the door opens, and she walks in.

Angela Guerra—*Ms*. Guerra—wasn't married to Karpe's father when I left town last year. She's young for a lawyer, maybe thirty, with long legs and a real short skirt. *Trophy wife*. The hated expression leaps to mind, watching the swing of her long, dark hair as she leads me to her office. But something about her tells me, Angela Guerra is no guy's trophy.

She closes the door. The office has a view of the bay. The sun glints off the water, blinding bright, so I look away, staring instead at the business card holder on her desk. I know from Spanish class that her name means both *Angel* and *War*. She doesn't say anything, waiting. For a second we have a staring contest.

I lose. "I'm here about the Lisa Monroe murder trial," I say.

"Oh?" Looking at her legal pad, like nothing's changed by my words.

"Yeah. Yeah, she's my mother."

A slight intake of breath. So Karpe didn't tell her. But she recovers and clears her throat.

"So, you're the missing person," she says.

I smile. "I once was lost, but now I'm found."

She doesn't smile back. "Julian said you had a sense of humor."

"I had one."

"What happened?"

"You know what happened. Everyone knows."

"They know what the newspapers say, what the lawyers choose to tell the newspapers. I'm a lawyer myself, so I know what we are."

"Liars?"

This time she does smile. "Oh, no. Lawyers—good lawyers—never lie. We tell the truth better than anyone. But whether we choose to tell *all* the truth— well, that's a different story. What I know is, you left. What I need to know is, why are you back? And why here, talking to me?"

Good question. I don't answer a second, considering the possibility of standing and heading back out the door I came in. Finally I say, "I'm not sure. I thought maybe you could help me."

"With what?"

With deciding what to do. With telling me whether being here will help my mother, or if I should stay a missing person forever.

I say, "I came back to Miami. I've been gone a year, and no one knows where I was." I wait for her to ask me where I've been, but she doesn't. "So I wanted to know if anyone's looking for me."

"Why would they be?"

"I don't know. To give information. To interview me

on CNN. Because I ran away, maybe, to put me in a home for messed-up kids."

She smiles. "Well, forget that last one. If the police spent their time looking for runaways, they'd never do anything else. I probably shouldn't tell you this, but I will. As long as you lay low, you can stay gone forever. And I get the impression you're good at laying low . . . if laying low is still what you want. Where have you been all this time?"

"I'd rather not say."

"I was just concerned about whether you're some-place safe."

"Safe enough." She keeps looking at me until I add, "It's just, why should I trust you? How do I know that what I say won't end up on *Inside Edition* or something?"

"I guess you don't."

"That's comforting."

"How do you ever know you can trust anyone? But everything you say here is protected by attorney-client privilege. You walked in that door, you became my client. You walk out, I can't tell anyone what you said unless you say it's okay."

I test her. "I'm a client even though I'm not paying you?"

She nods. "But I can't help you if you won't talk to me, Michael."

I look down. "Where I am, it's . . . complicated."

"People say I'm pretty smart."

"So smart you represent clients for no money?"

She doesn't answer that, and I know she's waiting.

"I've been traveling with the carnival," I say. "I started working there about a week before . . . before Walker died. And now the carnival's back in Miami, and so am I." I give her a look, like *that's it*.

"Right. Why did you leave home?"

"I had to get out of there," I say. "Every day I thought he was going to kill her, maybe both of us. It was like playing Hot Potato with a hand grenade. You never knew when he might explode. And she wouldn't leave. I tried to get her to ditch him, but she wouldn't go. I felt . . ."

Weak. The weight of the word is inside me. Like I have to make her, this stranger, understand or I can't go on. But I don't want to admit how weak I felt either. I mean, the problem should be that Mom was getting hurt, not how it made me feel, not how much I hated her for how it made me feel.

I glance at the door again. When I look back, Angela's looking at it too.

"Do you want to stay here?" she asks.

"Yes. No. I don't know. I guess . . . I want to know if there's anything I can do. If not, I should probably leave town before anyone catches me."

"And go where? Do you plan to stay with the carnival, just keep running away forever?"

"I can't think of a better alternative."

"I can think of several, including that group home you're so afraid of." She looked me in the eye. "Julian says you were a good student. Don't you want to finish school?"

"I wasn't that good a student. And I don't know what I want."

She glances out the window at Biscayne Bay. I think about how it's the first time I've seen the bay since I left last year.

When Angela looks back, she says, "It's all right not to know. It's okay to be afraid, too. But at some point you need to take a chance, let someone help you."

"I don't know if I can do that either."

She turns to the computer on her desk and pulls up a calendar program. "Is nine o'clock good for you?"

"Huh? Nine o'clock when?"

"Same time, Thursday. Does that work for you?"

"Yeah, but. . . ."

She takes her hand off the mouse and looks at me. "I want to help you, Michael. But I don't have time to sit here and *not* talk to you. It seems to me you need to do some thinking. Come back Thursday?"

Today is Tuesday. I nod.

"Same time?"

I nod again. She picks up one of her business cards, writes down the appointment, and hands it to me.

"Sometimes you need to have the guts to trust someone, Michael."

I take the card from her.

"I used to trust a lot of people," I say.

LAST YEAR

So the next day, after my attempted assault on Dutton, I was back in the cafeteria. It was St. Patrick's Day, a holiday that must have been invented by Bennigan's. The place was awash in every shade in the puke spectrum (worn by guys with Irish names like *Jose*), and the lunch ladies were serving corned beef and cabbage.

Irish eyes: Not smiling.

I should have worn green. Lately my efforts had been concentrated on blending with the crowd. Usually that meant jeans and some kind of T-shirt. But today, in my blue jeans and blue shirt, I stuck out like a buoy in a sea of green.

I was eating pb&j again. I'd brought three sandwiches to have something to do. I remembered this *Peanuts* strip where Charlie Brown says lonely people eat peanut butter, and if you're really lonely, the peanut butter sticks to the roof of your mouth.

I swirled it off with my tongue.

"You've got the right idea." Julian put his tray down across from mine. "I should bring my lunch instead of eating the stuff they sell here." He gestured toward his Styrofoam tray full of corned beef and cabbage. "What is this anyway?"

I ignored him. That was, after all, the reason I sat in

the cafeteria instead of outside: No explanations required here. Guys like Tris, they got mad if you didn't answer their questions. Someone like Karpe was so used to being blown off, he probably didn't even notice.

"Does your mom make your sandwiches?" he asked.

"What do you think?"

Karpe didn't react to my annoyance. That would have destroyed his credibility as a wannabe. "I think she did, lucky guy. At my house, it's just me and my dad. We eat manly meals in manly ways—we're lucky if we take the lids all the way off the cans of baked beans before we ingest them."

He laughed at his own joke. I'd never met Karpe's dad. When we were friends, he'd lived with his mom, a working mother like mine. I wondered now why he'd moved, but I didn't ask. Probably it was because of that "male influence" people always worry about.

In Karpe's case, it hadn't worked.

I considered enlightening Karpe that bringing a sandwich wasn't exactly my choice. Walker kept a tight leash on Mom, letting her buy groceries once a week with his ATM card, but policing her other spending so even a buck-twenty-five cafeteria lunch would be noticed. That's why I brought my lunch.

The weird thing was, I actually considered telling Karpe that—even if it was just for a second. Tris, or any of my other, more recent, friends, I wouldn't have told in a quadrillion years. I told myself it was because I didn't care what Karpe thought. But was it that?

I said, "Why are you sitting with me?" Karpe wasn't wearing green either.

"Hey, this was my table. I always sit here."

"Oh." I felt oddly disappointed, then wondered why. Was I so pathetic I actually worried whether Julian Karpe liked me? "Sorry. I could sit with my friends or something."

What friends?

"You can sit here. You're sort of . . . less of a jerk than your friends."

I laughed. "Oh, thanks. What makes you say that?"

"You make eye contact, for one thing. Guys like Ted Dutton act like they'd turn to stone if they looked at the wrong person."

"Okay, I'm superior to Tedder Dutton. Check."

"And, I don't know," he said. "You always picked me for your team in P.E., even after we stopped hanging together. If you weren't captain, I got picked last, except maybe a couple of really *slow* girls. But you'd pick me fourth or fifth."

More like sixth or seventh, but, yeah. I'd felt guilty about not being friends with Karpe anymore, so I'd picked him sometimes. And he always, *always* rewarded me for my generosity by striking out or fumbling or kicking the ball toward the wrong goal.

"That's so lame," I said. "Can't believe you told me that. It's humiliating, really."

"Yeah, I know." He played with his cabbage. "Doesn't matter, though."

"Don't you care what people think of you?"

Karpe shook his head. "People mostly think the same, whether you care or not." He took a bite of cabbage.

"So that's also why you don't care if that crap makes you . . ."

"Flatulate?" Karpe grinned. "It doesn't. I have excellent self-control—probably from eating all those canned beans with my dad." He took another bite of the gray slime and finished it before saying, "Why *don't* you sit with your friends anymore?"

"I just don't feel like it, okay? God, do you always ask questions like that?"

"You were the one who asked first."

I changed the subject. "Want a sandwich? That looks like toxic waste." I realized too late I sounded like Dutton. "I mean, I have an extra one."

Karpe nodded. I fished the third sandwich from my bag and handed it to him. Of course, that had to be the precise moment Tristan walked into the cafeteria. That sound you heard was planets colliding. Tristan hesitated, then came over. He looked first at me, then at Karpe. Then at the empty seat beside me.

"Hey," he said.

"Hey," I said.

Karpe opened the pb&j and rearranged the pieces of bread so one half was all peanut butter, the other half all jelly, oblivious or pretending to be. Tristan sat down, trying to ignore Karpe but not completely succeeding. He wore a mostly green University of Miami National Champions T-shirt.

"Missed you outside," he said, uncertain, like a dog on his fifth day at the pound.

I said, "Right. Like I could go back there again."

"You could. Dutton's used to people busting on him. He'd get over it."

"If he's such an asshole, why do you want to hang with him?"

"Well, it's . . . I mean, we have football together."

"Right. Football."

"You used to like football. You used to be okay with sitting with us too."

"It's not that. It's . . ."

I stopped. Why was I arguing with him? He was inviting me back. All I had to do was nothing, and I'd have a place to sit at lunch, people to talk to, parties on weekends. I wouldn't have to sit around worrying about whether Julian Karpe—Julian Karpe, for crying out loud, who couldn't even eat a *sandwich* correctly—liked me. It would be so easy. I might even be able to beg Coach to let me play football again. Maybe not first string. Maybe not even varsity. But play. Get my life back.

Easy.

Except it wasn't. Nothing was or ever would be easy again.

"It's what?" Tris said. "What is your problem?"

"Could you just . . . ?"

Go. Leave. But I couldn't get the words I wanted, and I was just so tired of saying what I didn't want. I was just so tired of all of it.

"It's okay," he said. "I can see from your face."

"What can you see? That you've turned into this loser who hangs with guys like Tedder Dutton like it makes you someone? Are you really this pathetic?" I knew I was being cruel. Still, I kept going. It was that same exploded Coke bottle feeling. Soon they'd hang a sign around my neck that said *contents under pressure*. "You should carry his books, Tris. Or do his laundry." I was gesturing wildly with my sandwich. "That's it. You've already got your nose up his ass. Why not sniff his jock, too?"

"Okay," he said. "I get it. At least now I know where I stand with you."

"Yeah. Yeah, you do."

"Fine." He stood and started to leave. But just then, three cheerleaders showed up. Vanessa—my luck—with two friends, Katie Gonzalez and Kiffani Stringer. They carried green-dyed carnations they were delivering for the cheerleaders' carnation sale.

I'd forgotten about the carnation sale. They were two dollars each, and I'd always sent them to potential girlfriends and just friends. This was the first time I hadn't bothered. It would suck if someone sent me some and I hadn't sent any to them.

"Special delivery for Tristan Kaboleusky." Kiffani held out an armful of green carnations and pushed out her chest, showing off her new cheerleader uniform.

"What's this?" Tris laughed. Tris had never gotten many carnations. He griped that girls told him he was "nice" or "a great friend" ("which means too ugly to consider," he said).

"We take care of our guys," Kiffani said.

"We're working on a cheer for you," Katie added. "Except we can't think of anything to rhyme with Tristan or Kaboleusky."

"Try *Grab a brewski*," he said.

"Time for class!" Karpe picked up his tray and my

trash and took them to the conveyor belt.

I left in the opposite direction. When I looked back, Tris was still talking to Kiffani. She had her hand on his shoulder.

I was glad, I told myself. Tristan was a good guy. I'd just grown past our friendship, while he hadn't.

Except part of me wanted to run back to the cafeteria and stand on the table and yell and yell until someone caught me and held me and took me away.

THIS YEAR

"Karpe?"

I make sure I call right after school, even though it means getting someone to cover for me and calling from a pay phone by the livestock tent. I want to get Karpe alone.

"Is that you, Michael?"

"Yeah. Listen . . . about Angela."

I stop. I want to ask if he's sure I can trust her. After visiting her office, I started thinking about what that meant, putting myself out there. She tried to persuade me to turn myself in, go into a foster home, for God's sake. And, even with attorney-client privilege, you hear about lawyers selling their stories all the time. I wasn't sure how that happened, but I knew it did.

"Yeah. You going to call her ever?"

"I wanted to know . . ." I stop. "She didn't tell you I came to see her?"

"No. You did?"

"Yesterday."

"She didn't say a word."

Something moos in the background, and I think about what Karpe said.

"You mean you just didn't see her last night or something?" I ask after a minute.

"Actually we all had dinner together. Since Angela and Dad got married, we do that a couple days a week, take turns cooking, that type of thing."

"No more baked bean cans?"

"Well, sometimes. Not as much. I actually sort of *like* baked beans."

"So you all sat down and had dinner, and she didn't mention she saw me?"

"Not a word. I guess she thought you wouldn't want her talking about your case. What did you want to ask me about?"

"Um, I . . . You know what? Nothing. I mean, you answered it."

LAST YEAR

I went to the fair with Karpe for one reason. It beat going home. Why I went back, that's a different story.

It sounds crazy to say that—that I went to avoid going home. After all, I'd done everything in my power, quitting football, ditching all my friends, all to *stay* home. But that day, a Thursday, was my sixteenth birthday. I could not spend it with Walker.

I was standing by my locker, feeling sorry for myself, when Karpe showed up.

"Hey, Michael-Michael Unicyle! Want to go to the fair?"

I considered letting Karpe know people would like him better if he didn't call them stupid nicknames. But first off, I wasn't sure people would. And second, who was I to judge?

So I said, "Don't think so."

"Why not? It's opening night."

"No flow."

"I've got passes." Karpe flashed two blue tickets. "I'll pay."

"It's not just admission. Once you get there, it's like a giant vacuum, sucking out money—food, games, rides. . . ." I stopped. I sounded like Walker.

"I said I'd pay. I'll drive, too." Karpe looked suddenly

desperate. "Come on, Mike, I've got no one else to go with."

It wasn't because I felt sorry for him. I didn't. But I started thinking about how it was my birthday. How pathetic was it, to go home and watch television like it was just a normal day. I slammed my locker door. "How do we get there?"

"I've got a brand-new Miata, just looking for passengers."

He expected me to react, an *ooh*, or maybe an *ah*. I said, "Got any change?"

"I told you, I'll pay."

"For the phone."

Karpe flipped me a cell with a Spiderman cover and headed for the door. I shoved the lock onto my locker, then dialed. I sort of stared at the keypad before hitting Send.

One ring. Two. No answer. We reached the parking lot. Dutton and Tristan were there with some girls. They leaned against Tristan's pickup. When Tris saw me, he raised an eyebrow.

I hung up and waited a moment. We passed them. The girl Dutton was with was Vanessa. She'd told everyone in school I was an asshole. I hadn't defended myself.

"Looky there—Daye's got a new friend." Dutton

made Loser *L*s on his forehead.

"Aw, leave him alone," Tristan said.

I dialed again.

Mom answered on the first ring after my redial. "Michael, is that you?"

She knew it was. Walker didn't let her answer the phone when he wasn't home unless it was his number on caller ID. Sometimes, he tested her. So we had a code. Two rings, hang up, then ring back.

"Yeah, it's me," I said.

"Sorry. I was outside. I couldn't get to the phone."

Like I didn't know the truth. "Yeah, I know. Look . . ." I moved Karpe's phone to the other ear, away from him. "Look, I'll be late tonight. Tell him I have something for school."

"Oh, please, Michael. No. You know how he gets. I can't lie to him anymore."

No mention of my birthday, of course. Just Walker. And then, in the background, a door slamming. Walker was home early. "Lisa, who you talking to?"

"No one, honey." And the sound of the telephone being replaced, soft but quickly, in its cradle.

We reached the famous convertible, and I tossed the Spidey phone at Karpe. "Thanks."

He was looking at Dutton and those guys, but he turned to me. "Say, Mikey Boy, why are you always so broke? Thought your mom married some rich guy."

And I said, "None of your damn business."

But I still went with Karpe. It was better than the alternatives.

• • •

When I was a kid, the fair was like magic. Sometimes I'd go with Mom and whatever guy was trying to impress us. Other times it was just us. Those were the best, even though we couldn't afford wristbands that let you on all the rides, and we had to smuggle in our own sandwiches and soda. But with Mom, I could watch the shows and hear the music and not have to worry about owing someone.

Owing someone was a big part of the problem, going with Karpe.

"It says here there's a circus at three thirty." Karpe pointed at our complimentary program. "And every hour on the half hour after that."

"Negative." I kicked a half-empty cup of cherry slush in my way. "It's not a real circus. Just poodles, walking on hind legs and stuff." Though, even as I said it, I remembered how I'd loved it when I was younger.

"Oh." Karpe looked at the program again. "How about rides? The Doppel Looping goes upside-down twice."

"Rides are for kids."

"We are kids. What's up your butt?"

I ignored him, watching a guy with an American flag and the words, *My Country ~ Love It or Leave It*, tattooed on his arm. He held a beer bottle, circling the Whack-a-Mole game.

"Easy," the guy said to his girlfriend. "They gotta give a prize each game."

"But there's no one playing," she said.

"That's what makes it so easy."

His girlfriend gave the tattoo a squeeze, and the guy handed a dollar to the girl running the game. She stuck it into her money belt and pulled out an orange balloon. I watched as she fitted it over the nipple of the game and handed the guy a mallet.

"What do you want to do?" Karpe's voice, always on the verge of it, reached full whine.

"So, start," the guy commanded the Whack-a-Mole girl.

"I need four players." The girl held up four fingers. She wore leather bracelets on each wrist. She yelled to the nearly empty midway, "Three more players. Put the mole in the hole! Prize every time."

"Want to play?" Karpe asked.

"To win a stuffed Clifford the Dog? Not likely." I started to walk away.

"Well, I'm playing." Karpe went over to the Whack-a-Mole, waving a dollar, so I had to stay.

The girl took the money, barely glancing up. "Two more players! We're looking for terminators," she purred. "Whack-a-Mole exterminators!"

"Ain't no one here." The tattooed guy took a swig of beer.

"Sorry, sir. I'm not allowed to start with less than four players." She pointed to a sign that said that.

Something about her voice—or maybe the *sir*—caught my attention. I looked at her.

Because, you know, I hadn't before. Not really. I thought I knew what to expect. I'd been to enough fairs to know what a Whack-a-Mole girl looked like.

I was wrong.

First, she had no visible tattoos, scars, or body piercings. No scabs either. Nothing, in short, to ID her body if it was found in a canal. And she was young, nineteen or twenty. And pretty. Not the carnival kind of pretty that gets in your eyes like too much sun—just regular pretty. I felt like I'd seen her before. She repeated the balloon process. This time it was a green balloon. As she concentrated, a half inch of pink tongue slid out between her teeth. Her dark hair fell over her eyes so I couldn't see them. What I could see, at least if I walked closer, was the view down her green T-shirt.

I walked closer.

She finished the green balloon and stepped back.

She pushed the hair from her eyes. They met mine. They were brown. She held my gaze a moment, then looked away.

"Two more players!" she called. "Two more!"

"Start the game!" the tattooed man snarled. "There's no one else going to play."

"Maybe the lady wants to play?"

"I ain't paying twice for a shot at one prize."

"Pretty good shot, I'd say." The girl glanced at Karpe, who held his mallet like it might bend over and take a bite of his arm.

The guy grumbled but tossed her another dollar. He yanked his girlfriend toward him. "Now, start!"

The Whack-a-Mole girl turned and yelled into her microphone, "One more player for a chance at the prize. Second win gets you a big prize."

This time the balloon was yellow. But her eyes were still brown, the T-shirt still green. Unbelievable how everything in the world, everything in your *head*, can evaporate in a second over a hot girl in a green T-shirt.

I stepped closer.

The guy slammed the bottle on the counter. Beer splashed up onto his girlfriend.

"She needs another player, Les," his girlfriend said.

"Who asked you?" The guy raised his hand. The girlfriend flinched. Then, fast as it had happened, he turned back to the Whack-a-Mole girl. "Start the game *now*."

I was in this now. My fist was clenched, my heart racing. I hated bullies. Neither the guy's girlfriend nor the Whack-a-Mole girl seemed to mind, but I did. Beating the guy senseless—my first instinct—wasn't really an option, considering he was twice my size and twice my *mean*. If there was one thing I'd learned in sixteen years, it was that mean people always won.

"One more player! One more!"

"I'll play," I said.

I expected her to look grateful or something, but she didn't. I nudged Karpe to give her a dollar. She took it.

She gestured that I should stand by a station that already had a balloon attached. A purple one. She started the game.

I raised my mallet and began pounding, pounding, pounding. In front of me, it was this little mole, trying to pop out of its mole hole to safety. But in my head it was everything else. Mom, sitting with her hand on the telephone, afraid to pick it up. *Boom!* People at school, who used to be my friends, but now they crapped on me. *Bam!* Dutton, holding his fingers up in the shape of an *L. Boom, bam!* Karpe, pathetically begging me to come here, and my coming. *Boom! Boom! Boom!* Walker, hitting my mother. *Bam!* Me, never doing anything about it.

Pop!

And I was still pounding, pounding, pounding. And someone touched my wrist.

"Hey."

A few more bashes.

"Hey!"

I stopped. I stopped and looked into the eyes of the Whack-a-Mole girl.

"Hey. You won."

Below, the mole had gone into his hole forever.

"You won," the girl whispered again.

And the warmth of her hand, the intensity of her gaze, it startled me.

Karpe clapped me on the shoulder.

"Michael-Michael Row the Boat Ashore." *Clap, clap, clap.* "You won."

But I just saw the girl. "It's my birthday," I said.

Why'd I say that?

But she seemed to know. One hand, the hand not on my wrist, came up and grazed my cheek. Then she pulled me toward her, my mouth toward her mouth. And, around us, there was nothing. No shards of purple balloon, no spilled beer. No Karpe. No moles. Only her, her face, her lips, the feel and smell, the taste of her.

"Happy birthday, Michael." I watched her lips form the words. "Sweet sixteen?"

I nodded.

"And been kissed?"

"Yeah . . . thank you."

And, stupidly, I added, "My name's Michael."

"Kirstie." Then, "My break's at six. You could come back then if you wanted."

Not really a question. I nodded.

I let Karpe have the stuffed dog.

THIS YEAR

"Can I speak to Kirstie?"

"Who?"

"Kirstie Anderson?" But I already know the answer.

"Sorry. No one here's named Kirstie."

"Thanks." I hang up and cross the eighteenth *K. Anderson* off my list.

LAST YEAR

After Kirstie's kiss, Karpe and I left the game area. I promised to return at six, Kirstie's break.

Six. Two hours still. But I let Karpe lead me to the Tilt-a-Whirl, Das Funhouse, Doppel Looping. We even went into the tent with the one-ring circus. It was trained dogs, like I'd said, French poodles in ball gowns and bullfighter outfits. When they finally finished, the ringmaster announced the next act: "And now . . . from the jungles at the outer reaches of Mongolia, performing astounding feats of strength and flexibility, please welcome ten-year-old Ni-Jin."

She was a tiny thing in a spangled leotard, bending her legs back over her head, standing on one hand, then on a stick held between her teeth. Was she really from Outer Mongolia? Was Outer Mongolia even *real* anymore? And did it have jungles? Was she a captive, brought to perform for American carnival goers? Or was she just a regular schoolgirl with a really weird hobby? Had she been kidnapped, or did she escape?

When we left, I looked at my watch. Five fifty-five.

Karpe saw me look. "Got plans?" he asked.

"Wouldn't you?" I laughed. "Do you mind?"

"I'd do the same thing." He laughed too. I was starting to like him a little better, maybe even remembered why we'd been friends before.

"Hey," I said, "thanks for taking me here."

"No biggie."

When we reached the Whack-a-Mole, a game was in progress. I watched a guy in an exterminator's uniform win a stuffed bear for a kid. Kirstie didn't look at me, just handed the boy the bear.

She glanced up, smiling, like she'd known I was there all along. "Ready?" She unclipped her money belt and tossed it to an older red-haired woman who'd joined her.

"Yeah," I said.

Kirstie looked at Karpe. "You coming too?"

Karpe shook his head. "Think I'll try and upgrade to the big prize." He waved Clifford at her.

Kirstie smiled. "We'll be back in an hour." Then she leaned over and whispered something in his ear.

She saw me looking and said, "Excuse me."

"Sorry."

"That's okay." She gestured for me to follow her toward the midway.

"Where are we going?" I said. "Eat?"

"You hungry?"

"No." Remembering my suddenly empty pockets.

"Me neither." She was still walking fast, but she swung her hand, brushing mine. The second time she did it, I grabbed her fingers. She smiled, and I wondered why I was being so shy. We'd already kissed, for God's sake. But I couldn't decide whether to pull her toward me or pull back.

I pulled back. "So, where are we going?"

"Double Ferris wheel. I love it up there."

I nodded and followed her. I *was* hungry. But, more than that, I wanted to be with her.

The fair has a music of its own. Not just the music on the loudspeakers, heavy metal from the Himalaya, Garth Brooks from the fried-onion booth. There was other music, the call of the carnies, the whir of the roller coaster, the cries of kids begging parents for more tickets. I heard it. I heard it and felt Kirstie's nearness as we walked toward the ride.

We passed a booth, one of those spinning wheels where you pay a dollar for a chance to win something. A crowd of kids stood around, and the guy was about to spin it. Kirstie stopped to watch.

"You want to play?" I asked her.

She shook her head. "No. I don't believe in luck."

The guy spun the wheel, and it landed on *Lose*. Kirstie shrugged, and squeezed close to my arm. We headed across to the double Ferris wheel.

She strode to the front of the line and nodded to the skinny blond kid operating it. He let us in with the next group, Kirstie merging in so expertly that no one noticed we'd cut. We reached our car, and she waited while I pulled the metal bar down over us.

"That's Cricket." She gestured toward the blond boy.

"How old is he?" He looked twelve.

"That's not something you ask around here. People's real names, where they're from. Stuff like that's on a need-to-know basis. There's a lot of secrets around here."

"What's yours?"

"Maybe I'll tell you someday."

Someday. The word held a promise. And an irony, too, that she would kiss me but she wouldn't tell me her secret. It was okay. I wouldn't tell her mine either.

"Tell me something else then," I said when the ride lurched to a start.

"What?" She leaned toward me. Could have been the momentum of the ride, but I didn't think so. "What do you think you need to know?"

"What did you say to Karpe . . . to my friend?"

She smiled, and for a second I thought she wouldn't answer.

But she said, "I told him to pick the spot with the oldest-looking balloon."

"Why?" I remembered her putting on a new balloon for each customer, everyone but me.

"When you first put on a balloon, a new one, it's fresh, strong. But once it's been played a few times, it gets stretched out. There's only so much it can take. It's at the breaking point."

The breaking point. I thought about that. Then I thought about Mom in her beautiful, spotless house.

I said, "So you let me win."

"You could say that."

"Why?"

I thought she'd say she was grateful to me for playing, for rescuing her from that asshole. I *hoped* she'd say I was too hot for her to resist.

Instead, she moved closer. "You looked like you needed to win something."

"Yeah?" I edged away, but not too far. "So it was a *mercy* win? How about the kiss?"

"What about it?"

"Was it a mercy kiss?"

"You looked like you needed someone to kiss you, too."

That made me laugh, but sort of pissed me off, too. "You always walk up to guys you don't know and kiss them?"

"It's none of your business who I kiss," she said, drawing away.

I stopped laughing. As soon as the words left my

mouth, I'd known I sounded like Walker, calling Mom a slut or something. "I'm sorry. I didn't mean it that way."

She relaxed. "I know you didn't. It's just . . . so many guys are like that, like the guy tonight with that girl. I didn't think you would be."

"You really didn't know, though."

"I thought I did. I saw how pissed off you were, watching him. I just wanted to . . . I've never done that before, kissed someone like that. I mean, don't get me wrong—I'm no angel. I've done stuff I'm not *thrilled* about, but I've never . . ." She fidgeted her hands in her lap. "Michael, do you believe in destiny?"

"What?" But I'd heard her fine.

"Destiny. Ever meet someone, someone new, and know there was something going to happen between you—something good, or even something bad. But something that has to happen?"

I nodded.

"I saw you there," she whispered. "And you had to win so we could meet. I knew it. I don't *let* people win. My game isn't gaffed. But you had to win. I had to meet you."

If some other girl had said that, I'd have laughed. Destiny. How dumb. How overly romantic, like when girls see you at school and build this whole fantasy life around you and write notes to their friends without knowing one real thing about you.

I didn't laugh when Kirstie said it. I took her hands in mine. She let me.

But who knew what it meant to her, someone like her? *Some things I'm not thrilled about.* Maybe she met some guy who was her *destiny* every night, or in every town.

And part of me wanted not to care. But the rest of me smiled when she said, "I never felt that way before."

We sat there a moment, saying nothing, and when the ride reached its crest, she pointed out into the night and said, "Look."

"Look at what?"

"At everything." She spread her arm to indicate it. "Isn't it beautiful? Flat places like Florida the double Ferris wheel's the highest thing for miles. So you get up here, you can see forever."

"Flat places?" I said. "What about other places?"

"I worked a carnival in Seattle once. In Washington there's a mountain, Mount Rainier, that you can see a hundred miles away, even from the ground." She looked at me. "You've never been anyplace else?"

"Kennedy Space Center with my class at school once."

She laughed. "Last time I looked, that was still in Florida."

"Right." I looked away.

"Hey," she said. "I didn't mean . . . I mean, before I started traveling with the fair, I'd never been anywhere either."

"And now?"

"I used to keep a map with me, X out all the states I'd been to. A few times—like with Kansas City, Kansas and Missouri—I cheated and walked across state lines just to say I'd been there. But after a couple of years, I'd been in just about every state, except Alaska and Hawaii. I'd like to go to Alaska someday."

"And where's home?" I asked.

The wheel had made most of a rotation, and we were near the top again. She pointed at something. When I looked, I realized it was clusters of trailers, lined up like molars, hidden behind the rides. I'd never noticed them all the times I'd been to the fair before, even though they were in plain view. "That's home now. That's where I live."

"But, I mean, before that?"

"Another town, a little north of here."

"But I meant . . ." I stopped, remembering what she'd said about need to know, about secrets. Who knew what she'd run away from to come here. "Tell me about Mount Rainier," I said instead. "I've never seen a mountain. Is there really snow at the top all year long?"

She smiled. "Yup. And little waterfalls all over that you can find just by hearing them. And animals hiding, but you can see them if you walk quietly. It's really pretty."

I leaned and kissed her. It was different than her kissing me. Different than kissing other girls, too. I'd kissed plenty of girls at parties after football games, had some girlfriends, even done some stuff before Mom married Walker and it all fell apart. But somehow I felt like Kirstie knew what it was like to stand in the middle of a crowd and still be all alone.

I kissed her again now, on that double Ferris wheel that turned and dipped, turned and dipped, until I couldn't tell if the feeling in my stomach was motion sickness or maybe longing.

Below, Cricket was letting people off the wheel. I reached for the grab bar, still dazed.

"Are we getting off?" Kirstie said.

"Ride's over. I thought . . ."

"Do you want to get off?" she said, then smiled at the double meaning. "Do you want to get off the *ride*?"

The sun slipped behind the funhouse. It left a gray-streaked outline of itself. The fair lights were up, pink and green and blue. The lights were loud and the fair music was louder, and Kirstie's hands, her hair, her word, *destiny*, all stayed in my ears, shutting out

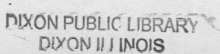
DIXON PUBLIC LIBRARY
DIXON ILLINOIS

everything else, all the bad stuff.

"No," I said. "No, I do not want to get off this ride."

That night Kirstie told me about Mount Rainier and the Mississippi River and all sorts of places she'd seen and I hadn't. And then my mouth was on hers again, not caring about, not knowing who was watching or what they thought, and all the fair music, the sounds, and lights, and smells gave way to one song:

You were meant for me,
And I was meant for you.

I never wanted to get off the ride.

• • •

When I got home, the light in the kitchen was on. I went to turn it off.

A voice stopped me.

"Happy birthday, dear stepson," it sang.

Walker. My radar was going nuts. Walker in a good mood, his face like a big, pasted-on smiley face, and almost as real. My every instinct screamed flight. But that wasn't the right thing to do. Instincts were all wrong here.

"Happy birthday to you," he concluded.

I turned. "Hello, Walker."

Did my voice shake? He stood, back toward me, by the table. He was still dressed from work, in a gray suit so expensive and clean it gleamed like a knife in the fluorescent light. Smoke curled around his balding head. He turned.

"Out late celebrating?" Still pleasant.

"Yeah." I huddled closer to the doorway.

A frown.

"I mean, yes. Yes, sir."

"Your mother said it was your birthday." Like he'd meant to throw a party. "How old?"

"Sixteen." *You bastard.*

"Sixteen . . ." Walker took a long drag on the cigarette, then released a puff into my face.

Don't react.

"And never been kissed?" he said.

"Can I go to my room now?"

"No." Walker took another drag. "Hey, I'm just trying to talk to you."

"Right."

"You didn't answer my question."

"What?" But I remembered and gave in. "Yes. Yes, I've been kissed."

"Wouldn't have thought so, Mama's boy like you."

Which I ignored.

"Been laid, too?"

Which I couldn't.

"No, sir."

"Good. Women are nothing but problems. But

you've got a girlfriend? Or maybe a boyfriend?"

I looked away. A small ant, the kind Mom called a sugar ant and said you couldn't get rid of no matter how hard you cleaned, made its way up the door frame. Did Walker see it? Not yet. But he would. I thought about the best way to kill it without Walker freaking out.

"You dumb, boy?"

"What?" I shifted from foot to foot, and as I did, moved my hand up to cover the ant.

"You don't like me much, do you?"

I squashed the ant, my eyes never leaving Walker's.

He continued. "Why don't you like me? You're such a crybaby. You get all whiny about a few everyday arguments."

Rolling the ant corpse between my fingers, then dropping my hand to my side, I looked at Walker, and the just-being-friendly expression on his face. I wanted to blow him away.

"You think you have it so bad here?" He swept his hand across the kitchen, taking in the dark wood cabinets, the top-of-the-line appliances. "You don't know what bad is. I grew up in a shack. Two rooms, and my daddy owned both of them. He used to set his shotgun sights on my mama when she cleaned house, made sure she did it right. Couple times he even pulled the trigger, came this close to blowing her brains out." Walker held two fingers up, touching one another. "Think we went crying to the authorities? They'd have laughed their asses off. We helped her clean the mess. That's just the normal way things are."

The normal way things are. I stared at Walker, wondering if this was a warning of things to come. Wondering if he had a gun, if he'd use it. I looked down.

"I want us to get along, Michael. I'm not a bad guy."

"Sure."

"You didn't answer my question. Again."

"What was it?"

"You got a girl?"

I shrugged. Before Walker, I had girlfriends. I had a life. Now my life was avoiding Walker and his bad moods, nursing dreams about leaving home, which I could not do. Staying from some bizarre idea of protecting my mother, which I could not do either. Mom and I had been close before. Friends more than parent and child, but close. Since Walker, though, I'd found myself hating *her* almost more than I hated him. Because he wasn't my parent and she was. Because she didn't understand what it was like to watch. Because sometimes my escape fantasies were so twisted I even scared myself.

"Yeah," I said. "Yeah."

Walker smiled and drew a bill from his wallet. "Take

her out someplace. On me."

The bill was new. So sleek and crisp I thought it might cut me, and I didn't want to take it, like some grateful beggar, taking his handout. But I did. A ten, cheap bastard. Still, I folded it in half, pocketed it, and started toward the door.

"Thanks," I said.

"No problem."

I opened the door, still feeling the ant corpse on my hand, the bill in my pocket, and hearing Walker's words.

"Your mom and I could use some time together."

I walked through the darkness to my room.

THIS YEAR

"You showed up," Angela says Thursday morning when I walk into her office.

"Yeah, I'm a little surprised I did."

"I'm not. You seemed like a smart kid."

"Coming here means I'm smart?"

"Knowing when you need help means you're smart. Also, your choice of attorney was brilliant." She leans her chin on tented fingers. "So now, tell me why you're here."

I glance out the window. I can see the Rickenbacker Causeway bridge, and if I followed it, I could almost find Walker's house. I look back at Angela.

"I've been thinking about my mother a lot," I say. "All the time, really. I want to know if there's anything I can do . . . to help her. Maybe talk to her attorney or the police. Can I do that without giving myself away? I don't want to go to a foster home."

"You probably couldn't."

Her words are like a door, slamming shut. I remember what she said about leaving the carnival, about not running. But I'm not sure I'm willing to give it up yet. I won't give it up for nothing, that's for sure.

"Will it help my mother if I talk to them?" I ask.

"That would depend what you have to say."

I pull a newspaper clipping out of my pocket, one I swiped from the library yesterday. It's just like all the others, calling my mother a trophy wife and a gold digger, making it sound like she married Walker for his money, then bashed his brains in to get her hands on it. The idea of my mother bashing anyone's brains in is impossible to me. And this article says Walker was planning to leave her. As if.

I say, "Know what the problem is with being a trophy wife?"

Angela smiles. "I can think of several."

"The problem is you get the kind of man who *wants* a trophy wife." I gesture at the article. "I want to tell them this is bullshit! They've got it all wrong. She wasn't the bad guy in this. He was. He beat her. He terrorized us . . . her. And even days he didn't, even when he was in a great mood, there was always the threat of it, always. We never knew if he'd come home with roses or a shotgun or what."

I remember my mother that day on the balcony, afraid to step onto the sand for fear of missing Walker's call, because of what he'd do if she wasn't there, waiting. Now I think if I'd only gotten her down onto the beach, I could have gotten her to leave him. But I didn't. I'd failed. She was trapped like a minnow in a tidepool, and I never did anything to get her out.

Until now. I glance at the ocean again.

Angela's voice interrupts me. "And do you think that will help?"

"I don't know. You're the lawyer. Don't they cut you a break if you kill someone before they kill you? Self-defense or something like that?"

"If it *is* self-defense. But it's hard to claim self-defense if you knock someone on the head from behind."

"She didn't . . ."

"The fatal blow was struck from the rear. You didn't know that? That's the big problem everyone's having with her self-defense claim."

I look away, picturing it. "He was a monster. Killing him was a public service. No one should be in jail for it."

"See, that's exactly the kind of thing you don't say to lawyers. Your mother killed a man, Michael. She freely admits she did it. Her options are limited. There's only so much you can accomplish. You need to decide whether it's worth putting yourself on the line."

"She doesn't belong in jail."

"You may be right. And this guy sounds like a total slime. But—"

"I *am* right. I can't handle . . . I mean, I was out of there. I'd escaped. But I can't go on like nothing happened. I can't stand that she's in jail for this. She doesn't belong there. She's not like people think she is. She's just . . . weak."

For the first time, Angela's face changes. She stands like she's going to walk toward me, but she doesn't.

"I understand," she says.

"You couldn't possibly."

"Okay. That's fair. But I sympathize. It must be hard, living with that."

"I'm not worried about me. I'm worried about her. What's going to happen?"

Angela sits back down. "There will be a trial. You know that. Your mother's confession means the state doesn't have to prove she did it. At first she tried to claim self-defense, but with a blow from behind . . . so her attorneys are defending her based on battered-spouse syndrome instead. That's saying that his abuse of her was so severe, that she felt so trapped, like the only way out was to kill him before he killed her."

"Exactly," I say.

"Exactly. But people—and juries—are suspicious of battered-spouse syndrome. We don't want to believe a man can trap a woman like that. We all believe *we* would be able to leave if we were in that situation."

"Do you believe that?"

Angela doesn't answer, and I say, "People don't know what it's like. I could tell them what he did to her. I'm not the one on trial, so I could tell them."

Angela nods. "But there are risks, Michael. You talk about escaping—that possibility would be gone. They *would* put you in a foster home."

"I know it."

"The other thing is, after you told your side of the story, they'd get to ask you questions. And sometimes they can make the story look very different, even if you're telling the truth."

"What would they ask me?"

Angela doesn't say anything for a minute. Then she stands and walks toward me.

"You didn't like Walker Monroe, did you?"

"I already told you I—"

"Did you?"

She says it sharply, and I realize she's showing me what they'd do. Cross-examining me. I say, "No. I hated him."

"Hated him. Did you discourage your mother from going out with him?"

"Yes. I knew from the beginning that—"

"But she didn't listen to you, did she?"

"No."

"She married him anyway?"

"Yes, she did."

"And after they married, you said, they fought a lot, right?"

"I said he hit her," I say.

"You were home when this happened? You saw it? You saw him hit her?"

"Yes."

"Over and over?"

"Yes."

"But you didn't do anything about that, did you?"

"No. I couldn't."

"You couldn't." She steps closer. "You never called the police, did you?"

"No."

"Your mother and Walker Monroe were married for about two years?"

"Right."

"And during that time, you're saying they fought, what, once a week?"

"More than that. It might have been that at the beginning."

"Twice a week?"

"Probably."

"And you called the police how many times?"

The room is silent, and I stare at her. "I could never have—"

"I'm sorry. How many times did you say?"

I give up. "I never called the police."

"You expect a jury to believe that you, a devoted

son—and a football player—watched your mother get beaten up maybe a hundred times, and you never called the police once? You just sat and watched?"

"I didn't watch. I tried, but I couldn't . . . do anything." I feel like I might cry, but I swallow it.

She steps away. "You love your mother, right Michael?"

"Yes," I whisper.

"You'd say or do anything to keep her from going to jail, wouldn't you?"

I nod.

"No further questions."

She walks back and sits behind her desk.

"That's what attorneys do, Michael."

"So you're saying it's hopeless?"

"I didn't say that at all. I'm saying you need to be ready for it. You have to get rid of this idea that you're going to go in there and say, 'He was a bad guy. He deserved it,' and everyone's going to say, 'Oh, okay.' Unfortunately, the world is full of scumbags, and there are still laws against killing them. The state attorney will fight hard. If you get into it, you have to be ready to fight harder."

I think about that. Finally, I say, "Can you get me ready for it?"

"Maybe. It won't be a sure thing, but I can help prepare you."

The intercom on Angela's desk buzzes.

"Angela, Mr. Pereira's here to sign the documents you prepared. Can you see him a moment?"

She rolls her eyes. "Sure." To me she says, "Sorry. I have to take this—very rich, very codependent client. Just think about it a minute, okay?"

I nod. "I never stop thinking about it, actually."

LAST YEAR

The breaking point.

Five thirty. I woke with Kirstie's words in my head: *At the breaking point.* Then my mother's from last week: *He says he'll kill us both if I leave.* The words circled like turkey buzzards as I dressed soundlessly and brushed my teeth in darkness.

They circled:

. . . at the breaking point
He'll kill us if I leave
. . . at the breaking point
He'll kill us if I leave

Chasing each other until they merged together, becoming one sentence:

He's at the breaking point and he'll kill us if I leave.

I walked to the bus stop, trying not to think of Kirstie. I'd told her I'd be back that night, but I wouldn't. It had been okay last night. No one had gotten hurt. But I couldn't chance it again, couldn't let my dick—or even *destiny*—make my decisions for me. I couldn't go.

Yet I felt Walker's ten in my pocket, nudging me, saying I could.

The money screwed everything up. Before the money, I'd had no choice. Now I had a choice, a bad one: Go back to the fair, see Kirstie, and leave Mom home with Walker. Or stay home and hear him gripe—or worse—about my being there.

I couldn't go.

I walked along the seawall that separated our street from the bay. Kids around here climbed in to dip their feet, so the rocks were littered with soda cans and cigarette butts. Usually I liked walking around it anyway, first thing. It was peaceful.

But today, even before I reached the water, I heard the commotion, like fireworks below the surface. The water was leaping, churning, white and silver with something flying out of it. I stepped closer. The motion stopped, then started again a few feet away.

It was fish, dozens, hundreds, leaping to escape an unseen predator. They came out of the water an instant, then dropped back in.

I couldn't see what was chasing them, but I knew they were fighting to survive. They swam in schools all day, but dammit, when a predator hit, it was every fish for himself.

Then it stopped. The water was silent again, so still and blue I could see my face.

• • •

"Michael Daye!"

Miss Hamasaki's voice was sharp, so I knew it wasn't the first time she'd called on me.

"Sorry." A few snickers around me.

"What was the main theme of *The Great Gatsby*?"

Which, apparently, we were still reading in English class.

A few more snickers. Then some AWOL part of my brain made my mouth say:

"Destiny."

Miss H. looked surprised, and no one was even trying to hide their laughter anymore.

"Destiny?" Miss H's voice was far too gentle. "Why, Michael?"

Walker was right. I should have reread the book. I had no idea what it had to do with destiny—or why I'd said it. But now I was stuck.

Behind me, some joker started a low *Duuuuuuhhhhhhh*. Maybe it wouldn't be so bad, flunking out of school. I stared at the book cover.

Then the answer came. I said, "Daisy was Gatsby's destiny. He bought the house across from hers because he had to. He didn't have a choice, even if he was just going to stare at her green light across the water. It was what he was meant to do."

Miss H. was nodding. So, like nut jobs always are, I was encouraged.

"Gatsby was a pawn. He ends up taking the rap for something she did and dying for it. But it was okay. It was what he wanted, what he was meant for."

You were meant for me,

And I was meant for you.

"Destiny is worth dying for," I said.

No one laughed now. They stared, silent, like I'd said something scary. Maybe I had.

Miss Hamasaki was still nodding.

After class, she approached me.

"Are you all right, Michael? Is everything okay at home?"

No! I wanted to scream it. *No!*

But I remembered what happened when I told Mr. Zucker. I said, "I'm fine."

"Because if you ever need to talk, I'm here, Michael."

"I'm fine. Look, I'm late for history class—it's all the way across the building."

• • •

The rest of the morning I stared ahead, ignoring everyone like I did. That was until after fourth period, on the way to lunch, I ran into the one person who wouldn't be ignored.

"Michael-Michael Bo-Bichael!" a voice sang behind me.

"Yeah?" I stopped him before he could go into the *Banana-fana* part.

"Going back tonight?"

"Where?" I walked faster, not wanting to talk about it.

"Where?" Karpe imitated. "The fair, the scene of the crime." Karpe leaned toward me. "You'll get lucky tonight. I can feel it."

I could feel it too. Or feel something anyway. And I could hear Kirstie's words, *I never felt that way before.* I could almost see them, as if they were burned on the air by a skywriter.

But I kept walking toward the cafeteria. Problem with Karpe was he didn't take a hint. Most people—most normal people—if you ignored them, answered their questions with single words, sped up when they tried to walk with you, they bought a clue. Not Karpe. He just sped up his own Frankenstein walk. Only thing that worked with guys like that was brutal honesty.

"Why don't you go?" I said. *As in, leave.*

But Karpe didn't get it. "Wish I could. That girl was finer than frog hair—but you're the one she's hot for."

Sometimes even that didn't work. We reached the cafeteria door. Though I'd hoped not to walk in with Karpe, that was obviously wishful thinking. So I held the door for him, let him get a head start. I lagged behind.

"Where we sitting, Mikey-boy?"

I took a single empty seat, away from where we'd sat

before. *"I'm* sitting here."

"Great." Karpe leaned toward the freshmen sitting in the seats across. "I'm sure these guys won't mind shoving over so we can brainstorm your next move." The freshmen, perceptively realizing the danger of arguing with a madman, shoved over. Karpe said, "I'll go buy my lunch." Then he was gone.

It was raining out, so the caf was more crowded than usual. My sandwiches were peanut butter and banana. I never used to bring that because they grossed people out. Now I didn't care. I *wanted* to repulse people.

A tray slid onto the table across from me.

"Back already?" I was almost looking forward to abusing Karpe some more.

But it wasn't Karpe. It was Tristan.

He wrinkled his nose. "Whatcha eating, Mike?"

I put down the sandwich. "Someone's sitting there."

"Since when is Julian Karpe someone?"

Since he didn't sit there with Tedder making Loser Ls at me.

"What do you want, Tris?"

Tristan fumbled with his spork, even though he'd gotten a hoagie. Tris was one of those hyper guys who always had to be doing something with his hands. Finally, he looked up.

"I don't know," he said. "I mean, I know. I mean . . .

114

what's up with you, man? You quit the team. You stop talking to everyone. You're picking fights, and then you're hanging with . . ." He kept struggling with the spork wrapper. "With Karpe, for God's sake. The guy is a Black & Decker power tool. And I heard about English class, you babbling about death and shit. What's with that?"

He poked the spork tines through the plastic, trying to rip it. I grabbed it and pulled away the wrapper. I held it out of his reach.

"What's your point?" I said.

"My point is, you used to be this perfectly normal person. I mean, someone you could have a conversation with. Now . . ." He reached for the spork. I played keep-away with it until he gave up. "Now you walk around here like some kind of terrorist. I hear the guidance counselors started a file on you in case you go postal and shoot up the school."

"Are you done?"

"No. I know you've decided I'm scum, but we've been tight since middle school. I had to . . . what's the deal, Mike?"

For a second I thought I should tell him. Like talking to Tris would make things All Better.

"Look," Tris said, "Alex Ramos is having another party Thursday. You should go."

"That's what this is about? A party?"

"Not just a party—*the* party. At his dad's place out in Horse Country. He hired a band, The Irritants, and they've got a pool, a hot tub, and—most important—no neighbors to complain."

"A party," I repeated.

Tristan sighed and reached for the spork. I gave it to him. "It's not about partying, Mike. It's about being normal again. I want you to come. Can you please come?"

What a joke. What did I think—if I told my *football buddy*, he'd swoop in like Spiderman and fix everything?

"Okay. You asked. You did everything you had to. Now leave me alone."

"Mike . . ."

"Get out of here!"

He left, and I went back to my peanut butter and bananas.

Bang! Bang! Bang! Karpe announced his return. He sat, taking a monster bite of his sloppy joe, then talked with food still hanging from his mouth. "So, what are we going to do with you, Mikey Mouse?"

"Nothing," I said. "I'm going to the fair."

• • •

Before I could go, I had to talk to Mom.

When I got home, she was pulling into her spotless

garage in the red Porsche, Walker's extra car that he let her drive the rare times he allowed her to go out. "Where were you?" I asked.

"Out." Breezy, staying in the car. "Walker made me an appointment at the Mandarin."

"The Mandarin?"

"The spa."

"Well, yeah. I know that, but . . ."

"We're going out tonight. Walker has an important dinner. The Bar Association chose him as Man of the Year."

She looked at me from the car's low seat. Her skin—fresh from a facial, I realized—looked smooth, bright as glass. Then a shadow crossed her face.

"Man of the year, huh?" I said. "They don't know him real well."

"Michael, I know he's not perfect. I know he gets a little crazy with work, a little—"

"I think you're the one who's crazy!" I slammed my hand on the car's window. "How can you just . . . sit here like nothing's wrong when he treats you like this? Treats *us* like this!"

"Please, Michael, I can't . . ." She looked at the window, at the handprint I'd left there, and I knew she wanted to wipe it off. She was waiting for me to leave, so she could. "Walker gave you money to go out tonight, he told me. Why don't you go have some fun for once?"

"Fun? Why don't I just go and let him strangle you?"

I didn't know why I kept going over and over this, when her answer was always the exact same no. But I kept giving myself hope that this day would be different, that she would realize. She wouldn't. We both stared at the handprint some more.

Finally, I looked away. My eyes locked on a hammer hanging on the garage wall.

I grabbed it.

"Should I smash it?" I yelled.

"What?"

I held the hammer a few inches away from the window, from my handprint. "Should I smash it? Is that what makes you stay with him? The clothes? The car? The trips to the spa?"

"No!" She was flying against my arm, her glass face broken now. "No!"

"If I smashed it, you'd have to leave. Wouldn't you?"

With my arm, I made a motion toward the window. She screamed.

I kept going. "You would, wouldn't you? He'd kill you if I broke it."

I felt something in my throat. I thought it was a sob, but I realized it was laughter. I tried another swing, and again, she pushed against me, her will stronger than I'd seen in months.

"Is that what you want?" she yelled. "To break things? To be like him?"

She stopped pushing against my arm. I could have smashed the window right then if I'd wanted. But I didn't. I wasn't like him. I couldn't be like him.

"Do you know what it's like," I said, "to go out, not knowing what I'll find when I come back? If you'll be gone, or . . . ?"

"I'm fine," she said, still keeping her eyes on my arm. "You should go tonight, Michael. Be a teenager. When I was your age, I didn't think of anything but cheerleading and getting away from Grandma Mavis to go to the beach. You shouldn't have to worry about me."

"Yeah, I shouldn't, but . . . how can I not?"

She reached into her purse and took out her beeper. "Take it. I won't need it. We'll be together, so he won't call. You keep it. Have fun. And if there's any problem, I'll page you."

"Right. Have fun."

She kept holding out the beeper. I realized I still had the hammer inches from the glass.

I dropped it and took the beeper.

THIS YEAR

"Why are you representing me?" I ask Angela when she gets back.

"Excuse me?"

"Why are you representing me? Why waste your time talking to me?" And then the question I've been turning over in my mind since the last time I saw her. "What's in it for you?"

She uncaps the pen she's holding and draws a circle on her legal pad.

"Julian asked me to see you," she says. "I wanted to make him happy."

I put up my hand. "Not good enough. I know Karpe, and he can be bought cheap. A nice birthday gift, a home-cooked meal, maybe a stick of gum or something—he's good to go. You don't need to spend hours with me to impress him. Next reason."

She sort of smiles at that. "I guess, it's an interesting case."

"Right. You're taking time away from your real clients, from Mr. Pereira and whoever else, and working for me for no pay because I'm interesting?"

"Yes, actually. I worked for the public defender's office when I first started practicing. Now I mostly do corporate stuff—safe, but boring. This is something different."

"Then why'd you quit the public defender's?"

"I got tired of representing guilty people. I hated using my very expensive legal training to think up an angle to get a suspended sentence for some guy who was caught selling smack in front of an elementary school. I understood why those guys were entitled to legal representation. I just didn't want to be the one doing it."

"So why do it for me?"

"Ah, that's an easier question. You're innocent."

I look at her a second and think about what she said the state attorney would ask me. I think: *Am I innocent? Am I really?*

I give up on my quiz. "I think what I need is to see my mother. Can I see her?"

She looks uncertain for the first time. "Are you sure you want to do that?"

"Will that be a problem?"

"Just . . . I guess I'm feeling protective of you. You say you can't handle the idea of her in jail. What about seeing her there? I'm sure she's changed a lot in a year. It could be quite a shock for you."

I sort of smile at that. "Angela . . . Ms. Guerra. It is really sweet of you to want to protect me from the awful truth. But, you see, I undid the ropes once when he tied her to the bed before he went to work." Angela sort of flinches, and I add, "And you want to know the really screwed-up part of it? After I untied her, she still made excuses for him, still gave me her b.s. about the sanctity of marriage and how if we didn't do stuff to upset him, he wouldn't get so mad. So when I got home from school that day, I had to tie her back up so he wouldn't find out."

"What was he so angry about?"

"He'd lost his keys and he was convinced she'd taken them. To leave him."

Angela nods. "I'm sorry, Michael. I know how hard it must have been."

"You don't understand. You don't if you think seeing her in jail would be too much for me. It's a lot better than seeing her dead."

She puts the cap back on her pen. "I do understand, Michael. I guess that's the other part of the reason I want to help you. I grew up in a home like yours. My parents used to fight so much, and I remember lying in bed, hoping the neighbors wouldn't hear because that was all that was left to hope for. That, and that I'd never end up like my mother."

I glance out the window now, at a boat going by. But really I'm picturing little Angela, cowering in her bed.

"So what you asked me just now—all that stuff about how I did nothing?"

"I knew you couldn't have done anything. I knew how crummy you must feel."

"But you kept asking me anyway?"

"You needed to know what you'll be up against in court."

I glance out the window. "What did you do?" I say.

"Do?" She seems surprised by the question. "I didn't do anything. I was six years old. And seven, and eight, and nine—and after the first hundred times it happens, you sort of know she'll never leave. This was my real father, so it had gone on all my life. I'm not sure I even realized leaving was an option. So I'd just lie in bed, waiting for it to be over until next time."

"No," I say. "I mean, what did you do, eventually, to get away?" I'm thinking about my friends at the carnival. There, stories like Angela's are common. So many carnies are running away from one thing or another.

But Angela smiles. "That's the good part. I grew up. I went to law school and lived my life and tried to forget. The day I graduated, I looked out into the audience and saw my parents sitting there, and I knew I'd gotten my wish—I'd never be like her. That's how I got away."

I say, "I want to see my mother, Angela. I need to talk to her. I think I have to find out what she wants me to do. And . . ."

"What?"

"I miss her."

Angela nods. "I'll take care of it."

LAST YEAR

"You look like my kid."

The guy running the hamburger stand was missing teeth, but that didn't keep him from grinning. I was at the fair again, minus Karpe, getting a burger for Kirstie, who was working. When she saw me, she'd smiled, but said, "You can't hang here while I'm working—hurts my business."

"How?"

She shrugged. "Gotta work the crowd."

"You mean come on to guys?"

"Something like that."

"Is that what you were doing with me last night? Working the crowd?"

"Don't be a child." Which seemed strange to say, considering she was, maybe, three or four years older. She brushed my hand with hers. "What do you think I was doing?"

And while I was thinking, she sent me off to get the burger. "Tell Hank it's for me."

"You're sure you're not my kid?" the burger guy—Hank—asked.

"What?" Not sure I'd heard him right over the music from the Tilt-a-Whirl.

"I got fourteen kids. Gets so's you can't remember

who's who. You just say, 'Hey, kid,' and see who shows up."

He looked at me, seeming to expect a response and not finishing the burger. So finally I said, "My name's Michael."

"I might have a Michael." He gestured at the onions—did I want any? I shook my head.

"Fourteen kids." Thinking about what Walker would say about that, about this man's contribution to the gene pool. "Do you see them all?"

"Every chance I get. They live in Mobile with their ma." He looked around. "But this ain't Mobile, is it?"

"No." Then, dimly remembering that Mobile was in Alabama, I added, "But it's the next state over. Maybe next week?"

"Nope." He added ketchup without asking. "Not going to Mobile next. Don't rightly know where I'm going, but it ain't Mobile."

He looked suddenly sad. I felt Mom's beeper in my pocket. It hadn't gone off yet. Maybe it was like when you took an umbrella, how it never rained then. I hoped so. I realized she hadn't given me her cell phone because Walker would have noticed. God, I hated Walker.

I said, "Why not get a job where you'd see them more, not travel?"

He shrugged. "Sawdust in the blood. I been doing

this since I was sixteen. Money's good. Just wouldn't seem right, staying in one place, laying brick or selling sneakers. No, this is the only life for me." He squinted at me. "You're sure you're not my kid?"

And for a moment I wanted to say, *Yeah, Dad. Yeah, it's me. Michael.* And join him in the family business. I wanted to be someone else.

But I said, "No."

Another gap-toothed smile. "Didn't think so."

I headed back toward the games, past the sign for racing pigs, past the fountain where a group of African acrobats performed contortions. I didn't remember much about my dad, but I think he had all his teeth. After that, it got pretty foggy. Mom said it was better not remembering. "I'd block him out too, if I could. But I'm too old."

I always laughed at that. Mom wasn't old. She was beautiful. And there were plenty of men around to notice. Men who took us to the beach, the movies, or the fair. One guy had even won me the big prize. But then there was the guy who'd locked me in the closet so I wouldn't bother him and Mom while they . . . and, come to think about it, it might have been the same guy.

I walked back and offered Kirstie the burger.

"I've hunted and gathered," I said, grinning. "Didn't know if you wanted onions."

"Oh, it's not for me." She leaned to take a dollar from an older guy—who got a long look down her tank top in exchange. "I can't eat from those grab joints all the time. It's for you."

"But . . ." The guy was still looking.

"You looked hungry."

I realized I was. I'd meant to eat before leaving home, but after talking to Mom, I just left. I glanced at my watch. After seven. Walker was home now. I touched the beeper in my pocket.

"Yeah," I said to Kirstie. "Thanks." It was weird, her wanting to take care of me like that. I realized I wanted to take care of *her*. I wanted to stop old pervs from drooling over her body, for one thing. Maybe I just wanted to take care of *something*.

Then, "Oops." She ran over to help a man on the other side.

When she came back several minutes later, she said, "Why don't you walk around a little, see the livestock or something? I'm busy tonight."

I glared at her, walking away, but only when I was sure she didn't see me. It was bullshit, her asking me to come back only to blow me off. I shouldn't stay. She was just a piece of ass among hundreds of other pieces of ass. I should go home.

But the wild midway music called me to stay. Stay.

I didn't go to the livestock tent, though. I went the other way, past the circus tent where Karpe and I had gone the night before. I considered going in, but decided against it. I'd only gone to make Karpe happy. Besides, it wouldn't be as real the second time. I walked past booths offering ID bracelets and massage-by-the-minute. I remembered the burger and took a bite. Then another, until I finished it and realized I was still hungry.

When I looked up, I was standing in front of the double Ferris wheel. I had no idea why. I recognized the guy, Cricket, who was working it. He beckoned me over.

"Hey, kid," he said.

"My name is Michael."

He didn't introduce himself. "Want to make a buck, Michael?"

"How?"

"The guy who was supposed to take tickets got here totally baked. Can you help me out there while I operate the ride?"

"I don't know. I'm supposed to be meeting Kirstie soon."

He snorted. "How can I say this? I'll pay you for the next hour, then you check with her. When she tells you she ain't ready, you come back and work some more."

Which sort of pissed me off, but I suspected he was right. Also, I liked the idea of working. I'd never been able to have an after-school job since Mom and Walker got married.

"What do I do?" I said.

"Take tickets, five apiece, and don't rip 'em. Just throw them in." He gestured toward a wooden box beside him.

I looked at my watch—seven twenty—and checked the beeper in my pocket again to make sure it was still on. But Cricket had walked away, and people were waiting. So I started taking tickets. At first I had to unfurl them and count them before I threw them into the box. Cricket was working the controls, making the seats come down so people could get on. And when the last seat came down, he hollered "Last one!" so I knew not to take any more.

After a few runs, I got so I knew what five tickets looked like, even if people handed them to me in a sweaty ball. I knew when the last person got on too, before the ride was set to run. And I started to stand like I'd always seen carnies stand, facing sideways and head down, not really looking at anyone.

That's why I didn't notice Cricket next to me at first.

"You get a rhythm going," he said. "So you can just stay there and think and *not* think, if you know what I mean."

I did. I looked at my watch. I'd been there almost an hour, and I hadn't checked my beeper since I'd first gotten there. Cricket was right. I couldn't tell you what I'd been thinking, but it felt good. Like when I was younger and I used to put up signs on trees and mow people's lawns for extra money. It had been a while since I felt like I'd actually worked for something.

The wheel was running regular, and Cricket pointed up at the highest car. "Look."

At first I didn't see what he was talking about. Then I did. A couple at the top of the wheel. The girl was riding, black tank top shoved up, her head in her boyfriend's lap.

"People think they're invisible up there. Or maybe they just don't care what we see." The car came closer until I could see exactly what they were doing. The girl was really young, maybe twelve or thirteen tops. Probably there with her parents and talked them into letting her go out on her own. The guy seemed older, my age. I looked away.

"You wouldn't believe the shit I see," Cricket said.

I thought he meant the night before. I said, "Kirstie and me, we didn't . . ."

"Yeah, I know you didn't," he said. "Kirstie ain't like that. She likes her privacy a lot for a carny. We screw with her about it all the time."

"Do you and she . . . I mean, do you . . ."

He laughed. "Yeah, she'd like to think so, huh? But no. I'm not crushing Her Kirstieness. But I love her, you know?"

I nodded.

Cricket looked at the wheel, and I followed his eyes to the couple from before. When I looked back at Cricket, he'd moved to the ride controls. He stopped it just as the couple reached bottom. They didn't budge.

I knew what he wanted me to do. I walked toward them. "Okay! Ride's over."

The girl started pulling down her shirt, quick, not making eye contact. Real young. The boy opened his eyes.

"Let us off last," he said.

"Sorry. You have to wait in line to ride again."

From the corner of my eye, I saw Cricket nodding toward a uniformed cop. He was standing about twenty yards away, collecting his free orangeade from a tired-looking orangeade wench. But before I had time to point him out, the girl climbed over her boyfriend. "Come on, Ian." She still didn't look at me.

I moved away.

When the ride loaded up, Cricket came back over.

"So you're, like, the morals police?" I said, laughing.

"Hey, you let people do that, they mess up the seats."
He laughed too. Then he got serious. "The marks,
the people in the real world, they think we carnies are,
like . . . what do you call those dudes in India no one
talks to?"

"Untouchables." I was surprised he knew that.

"Right. We're untouchables. But that's because they
don't see what's happening in their own clean little
world. The stuff that's going on in front of their own
eyes."

I thought of Walker and his Man-of-the-Year dinner,
and I knew what he meant.

Cricket fished out a crumpled ten. "Why don't you
check with Kirstie, then come back when she tells you
to bail?"

I did that. And when Kirstie told me to come back at
ten when the carnival closed, I almost didn't mind.

THIS YEAR

"Put the mole in the hole. Prize every time." It's five thirty Saturday. Only about forty hours until I see Mom. My guard is up, but I do my job. I focus on two girls in sorority jerseys and real short shorts. "I'm not talking pocket-sized junk either," I tell them. "We've got really *big* junk here."

One of the girls—the one chewing gum—giggles. "You're cute."

Her friend nudges her. "Lisette . . ."

"Hey, Lisette," I say, "ever play this game?" I know how to get money from girls.

"How old are you?" Lisette asks me. She has dark hair and looks a bit like Kirstie, if you don't look too close.

Her friend's still nudging her. "Lisette, are you trippin'?"

"Yeah, better watch out for me, Lisette." I grin, knowing how she'll react. When her friend looks away, I say, "I'm Robert. I'm nineteen. Want to try?"

Lisette hesitates. "Can I have a freebie?"

I shake my head. "Wouldn't be fair."

Lisette's smile tells me she's not mad, that, in fact, I have a shot with her. There have been a lot of shots this year, a lot of opportunities, both with other carnies and with townies who like to feel wild by making it with one of us. Kirstie once told me carnies sleep around so much because they're lonely . . . even though they're never alone.

"Does it help?" I'd asked Kirstie. "I mean, does it make you feel less lonely?"

"Nope," she said. "But you think it will, at first, so you try. Usually it makes it worse."

She was right. In the beginning I took a few girls up on their offers. But lately I've sat back. I've held back. Maybe I'm waiting for someone I love.

But for some reason—maybe because she looks like Kirstie—I say to Lisette, "I've got a break in an hour. See you then?"

And she says, "Maybe you will."

She walks away just as Cricket steps up. "Hold a sec," I say, and I start the game. Around me, they're all pounding. Cricket slips a copy of the *Miami Herald* in front of me.

"This guy looks like you, doesn't he?"

I glance down, knowing before I do that it *is* me, recognizing the photo, me and Mom at one of my games. Someone at school, maybe even Tris, must have snapped it, then sold it to the paper when the price was right. I hear the pounding in my ears.

"Since when do you read the paper?" I say. My throat hurts to talk.

"Some guy left it on the ride." He looks at it. "Is it you . . . Michael? His name's the same as yours."

"My name is Robert."

"But it used to be . . . look, you know I'm on your side. But it says . . . I mean, people might be looking for you. For this guy." He jabs the paper. "If it's you, maybe you were right. Maybe you ought to bail. You could get in trouble."

"It's not me!" But I grab the paper from him.

"Hey!" A voice interrupts. "Hello? Anyone there? I won. Where's my prize?"

"Sure." I walk away, still holding the paper and barely able to see the prizes through the blur from the ride lights and the haze of smoke from hamburgers burning.

Later, on my break, I go to the men's room and stare at the photo for a long time. Then I tear the article into little pieces and flush it down the toilet.

I forget all about Lisette until I head back to my joint and see her walking away, mad. I wish I cared, but I don't. There are only two people I care about in the world, and I can't be with either of them.

LAST YEAR

I left the double Ferris wheel at ten with twenty-five dollars in my pocket.

"Aw, you don't have to," I said, when Cricket handed me the money. "I'd have been here anyway." I tried to give the money back.

Cricket waved me off. "Fuggedaboutit. You work, you earn cash. That's life."

I pocketed it. It was mostly ones, and they felt heavy and good in my pocket. I raised a hand to Cricket and went back to find Kirstie. I was tired, I realized. Not sleepy but tired like I used to get after a football game.

Kirstie put me to more work, closing up her joint. While I pulled down the awnings, she finished counting her money and wrote the final figure on a slip for her money bag with a satisfied smile. I checked the beeper in my pocket. Still silent. But, of course, if Walker had my mother up against a wall, she wouldn't be able to call.

"I can't stay long," I told Kirstie. "It's late. I should get home."

"Early bedtime?"

"No."

"No," she agreed. "You're afraid something will

happen if you aren't there." Not a question. She tossed the money bag to a guy who came around collecting them, then came outside the joint to help me close up.

"What's your problem?" I said. "You tell me to come here tonight, then ignore me for hours. Now, when I have to go, you say stay. I just have school tomorrow. That's all."

She shrugged. "You want to go home, go home." She started to walk away.

I don't know if she walked really quickly or if I just sort of blacked out, but the next thing I knew, she was yards away, across the nearly empty fairgrounds, and I was listening to the thuds of my running shoes against the pavement, watching her hair, raven-colored, full of moonlight.

"Wait!" I said. "Wait for me. Please."

When she heard my voice, she stopped for me.

● ● ●

She took me back to the circus tent. It was a lot different than when Karpe and I had been there. Then there'd been hardly any audience. Now it swarmed with people, most of whom would have qualified for the misfit table if they'd gone to my school. I inhaled heat, smoke. A guy with tattoos all over, including his face, had a shouted conversation with his friend, who was over seven feet tall.

"Is there a freak show at this fair?" I asked Kirstie. I hadn't thought there was.

"They're my friends."

"I just meant . . . you don't seem like them."

"I am like them."

I was stammering out *I'm sorry* when Cricket showed up.

"What's the deal?" With Kirstie there, he ignored me. "We getting saved again?"

Kirstie laughed. "Not tonight."

"Good," Cricket said. "I been saved in Apopka and again in Savannah—and the season's just beginning."

Kirstie turned to me. "Every town or so you get do-gooders from some religious denominations who think it would be a new idea to try and convert the carnies."

"I got so many Bibles, I could make table legs out of them," Cricket added.

He laughed, but Kirstie said, "I hate them. They don't know anything about me, but they assume I need saving just because I'm here. I came to get away from that stuff."

"Hey, I came to get away from people beating the hell out of me," Cricket said. "That, and for the parties."

"Us against them," Kirstie said.

"Sleeping late. Eating an unbalanced diet."

"Not judging anyone, ever."

"Wild sex, cool drugs, free rides on the Himalaya," Cricket said. "That's the best part."

Kirstie glanced at me. "Michael thinks we're trippin'."

"No, I don't." I touched her fingertips. *Us against them*, she'd said. I used to be *them*. Now I wasn't, but I wasn't part of any *us* either. I was no one.

The guy with the tattoos came over and handed Kirstie and Cricket each a beer. He kissed Kirstie on the cheek. "A townie?" He gestured at me.

"'Fraid so," Kirstie said. "Stan, meet Michael."

"I'd make you happier."

Kirstie laughed. "Oh, I don't doubt it, Stan. I don't doubt it."

The guy walked away, and Cricket raised a beer to his back. "To irresponsibility!"

"To having nothing left to lose," Kirstie said.

"What does that mean?" I asked her.

"At some point, when you give up everything, there's nothing left to worry about." She handed me her beer. "It's freeing, in a way."

I raised the bottle. "To having nothing to lose!"

I moved closer to her, farther from the tightness of the group of strangers. Her hair smelled like outside, and I inhaled deeply. The girl from the show the night before, the contortionist called Ni-Jin, stood outside the circus ring, eating a hot dog and smoking. Up close, I could tell she was my age, not ten like they'd said. Then the ringmaster showed up.

He was still in his ringmaster suit, which is how I knew him. When he reached the center of the ring, someone yelled, "Now Bill's gonna talk."

"And talk," said another.

"Ladies and gentlemen," the ringmaster, Bill, announced. "Children of all ages."

I looked around to see if there really were kids there. There were a few, which seemed strange, considering the beer and booze and the way some of the women were dressed. I smelled pot, too, and thought about what Cricket had said about drugs.

"In the center ring," the guy continued, "Jack and Denise!"

A couple came in. The guy had on a suit that looked like he'd found it somewhere. The girl was dressed like a circus performer, in silver sequins and fishnets. She carried a bouquet of pink light-up roses they sold on the midway.

"What is this?" I asked Kirstie.

"A wedding," she said.

And, sure enough, the ringmaster started reciting, "Dearly beloved, we are gathered here to join Jack and Denise."

Denise did a little turn, displaying herself. She had a hot body, and some guys whooped.

"They're really getting married?" I said.

"For the season," Kirstie said. "Carny marriages go from, like, March to November, renewable after that. Some people have stayed together thirty years or more, season by season."

The ringmaster was saying, "Do you promise to love, honor, and not come home too trashed at night?"

"I love you, honey," Cricket joked by me, "but the season's over."

"Of course, if the guy beats the crap out of you," Kirstie said, "it's easier to clear out."

I thought about that. From what I could tell, lots of guys beat on women. Maybe most. I tried to think back on girls I'd dated. I'd never hit a girl. We'd mostly made out and, when we fought, it was about my not calling enough. This one girl, Ashley Cates, I'd dated in eighth grade, said I had a problem with intimacy. Where did girls come up with that stuff? I told her I didn't know what she meant, and she said, "Exactly."

Anyway, I'd never hit any girls.

"Does that shock you?" Kirstie asked.

"No," I said. "No one stays together anyway. My parents split up, and now I wish my mom would ditch my stepdad." I stopped. That was more than I'd meant to say. "What was your family like?"

"Let's just say I'll never get married, not even for a season."

"Did your parents fight a lot?"

"No," she said. "No, they didn't do that."

"What did they do?"

"Mostly didn't talk at all. I'd rather be alone than with someone who treats me bad."

"Yeah, me too." It was amazing, how much we thought alike. "Do you ever get lonely?"

"Yeah. Yeah, I get lonely."

I was going to ask something else, but she turned away. They were on the *I do*s.

". . . in fine weather or when you get rained out, for better or worse, until the end of the season or death, whichever comes first?" the ringmaster was asking.

"I do," said Denise.

"I now pronounce you man and wife."

That was it. Jack and Denise didn't wait to be told to kiss, just started sucking face right there. People whooped and cheered, then started heading outside.

"Where are we going now?" I said, glad to get out of the crowded tent.

"Double Ferris wheel," Kirstie said. "Traditional carny wedding night's spent at the top."

I flashed back to being up there with Kirstie, making

out. Then to the couple earlier. I looked at Cricket, and he was sort of grinning at me, like he knew what I was thinking.

"The whole night?" I said.

"That's how you know you're really married around here."

We followed the group outside. I realized I'd been holding my breath a little. Now I spread my arms out, feeling better. Cricket went to help Jack and Denise, then started the wheel up and let it make a few rounds. The fairground was mostly dark now, except for the ride lights against the black sky. I wanted to be up there, suddenly. I wondered how it would be, traveling with the carnival with Kirstie, together for the season at least.

I looked at her. Her dark eyes reflected the lights. "Thanks for bringing me."

"It's good, getting out of yourself sometimes." She squeezed my hand, then dropped it.

"Yeah." I turned to kiss her.

But instead of Kirstie, there was an old woman, older even than the people I'd seen when I visited Tristan's great-gramma at the Park View nursing home once. Her face was all wrinkles but her hair was black, pulled from her face like a ballerina's.

"This is Antonia," Kirstie said.

"The Amazing Antonia," the woman corrected.

"Hi, I'm—"

"No." Kirstie held up a hand. "Don't tell her. Let her guess."

"Guess?"

"That's what Antonia does here," Kirstie said. "She guesses."

I got it. "Oh, you're one of those people who guesses people's age and weight."

"Bah!" She waved her hand. "Age and weight is easy." She had some sort of accent. I couldn't tell from where. "I guess much more harder thing than that. There are some who say . . . I can read minds."

I laughed, then was sorry for it and put on a serious face. "Okay, what's my name?"

She held up her index finger. "One letter. I am always needing first letter."

"M." Not commenting that a real mind reader wouldn't need the first letter.

"Then, I guess Michael. And, for make good guesses, I guess you are sixteen and weigh one hundred eighty-two, give or take three pounds."

I'd weighed one eighty-four last time I'd weighed in, but my muscle tone was probably going. That was a good guess. I figured Kirstie had told her my name, for a goof. But I said, "That's great."

144

"Ask something else," Kirstie said. "Ask where you're from."

I shrugged. "Okay. Where am I from?"

The old woman touched my forehead and her own like she was really reading my mind. A few people were looking. Finally, she said, "Born right here?"

"Yes." I remembered telling Kirstie I'd never left Florida. I started to move away, but people were crowded around, watching like they were used to Antonia's routine. Again, I felt crowded like in the tent.

"Do another one," someone said.

Antonia did. "Occupation: Full-time student. You live with your mother, have not seen your father in, hmmm, twelve or thirteen years." She poked my upper arm. "You once play sports but haven't lately. Muscles, they start to go dead."

I pulled my arm away. "She told you that, huh?" I gestured toward Kirstie. I didn't remember telling her about my father, but maybe I had. I was ready to leave then. The old woman was a fake, but still, it was creepy.

She kept going, sort of staring off beyond the Ferris wheel lights, not at me.

"When you were, let me see, eight or maybe seven years old, you were trapped somewhere, no? I see dark. You are banging, screaming, but no one comes for too much time."

The closet. It had been the week before my eighth birthday. I'd been there hours.

"Since then, being trapped is what you fear most. Any tight place, an elevator . . . even a crowd, it bothers you. Am I right?"

"Yeah." I sort of choked it out.

"Until recently," she said. "Recently, your greatest fear is not of closed spaces, is it?"

I couldn't answer.

Kirstie touched the woman's arm. "Hey, Toni, Mike's supposed to ask the questions."

Others around, maybe seeing my face, started going, "Yeah." "Looka that, the kid's freaked out."

But I said, "What's my biggest fear now?" I held my breath.

The old woman turned and faced me. "Now your biggest fear is here." She tapped my forehead. "Inside you. It is anger, what anger will make you do." Her voice was a whisper.

"I have to get out of here." I shoved between Kirstie and the woman, then more, making my way through the wall of people. Some guys I shoved by looked pretty rough and pissed off. But I didn't care what happened. I just had to leave.

"It was a joke, kid!"

I turned. It was the old woman, but her creepy

accent was gone. Now she sounded like she was from Brooklyn or something, not a gypsy.

I stopped. "Did she tell you all that?"

Kirstie caught up with me then. I let her. But I could see from her face that, no, she hadn't told her. She hadn't known all that.

"It's my job, kid. I . . . guess. An educated guess, you'd call it like. Your name starts with *M* so it was probably Michael. Where you're from, I tell from your accent. Age and weight—that's an easy thing. I see thousands of people each day."

"But the other stuff? Like getting locked in the closet."

"Good, huh? That gets most people. All kids get locked somewhere, and they always remember. Watching you in the crowd, I could see you can't stand being closed in. That's all."

It was enough. It had to be. I couldn't ask about the other stuff. I couldn't. "That's all?"

"Except . . ." she said. The crowd around us had sort of backed away now, going off into the shadows, away from the light.

"Except what?"

"Except that last part. I give that 'trapped some- where' line all the time, and it always works. But that last part, I don't know where it came from."

"Which part?" But I knew.

"The part about being scared of anger. I never said that before. I just sort of . . . felt it, talking to you."

I looked at her. Was she screwing with me, playing with my mind because of how I'd reacted? I couldn't tell.

"I have to go," I said. I started walking away, not even thinking about Kirstie until she was running after me.

"She freaked you out, huh?" Kirstie said. "She does that to new people. Some carnies aren't very nice to outsiders."

"It's not that," I said. "Listen, I have to go home."

She caught my hand. "Are you coming back?"

I looked back at the group. I couldn't see Antonia anymore, but Cricket gave me a wave. I turned to Kirstie. Her hair was still shining, still full of the moon and the ride lights.

"Yeah," I said. "Yeah, I'm coming back."

• • •

When I reached home, after more than two hours on a train and two buses, the house was quiet. Mom's embroidered runner was on its table. Everything was fine.

THIS YEAR

I realize everyone here knows my name's Michael, from that night. From Antonia. They're calling me Robert because I asked them to. But they know the truth. I won't be safe here much longer. I don't even know if I want to be safe. It hasn't helped me this past year. And suddenly I feel just as choking-up breathless as I felt that night—*without* the crowd.

I go back to my trailer. Everyone else is out partying, but I have an appointment with Angela tomorrow. And Mom.

I pull the sheet aside and find another copy of the *Herald*. This time my picture's circled. Cricket's not the only one who's figured out who I am.

I bolt from my trailer and go to the pay phone. Even though it's after midnight, I know I'll try to call Kirstie.

LAST YEAR

In the next week, I spent as much time at the fair as I could. Mostly, I was with Kirstie. When she wasn't around, Cricket could usually find me someone who needed help and was willing to pay me for it.

It's weird to say that after quitting the team to stay home more, I spent so much time away. But I justified it by saying I didn't *have to* go to the fair like I had to go to practice. If I sensed a storm gathering, I'd stay home. I told myself that.

After a few days of this, Mom said, "See? You don't have to worry about me. He's really changing, Michael."

I didn't think so. It was like in football, you have hang time—that second or two when the ball's in the air and everyone's running, getting in place for the moment the ball descends. Walker had hang times, a few days, sometimes even a week, when nothing happened. But sooner or later the ball would be in play again.

"Be with your friends, Michael," she said. "It's easier."

I skipped a couple of days then, stayed home and had dinner with them, and missed Kirstie and Cricket, missed having some kind of life.

And nothing happened.

The third day I went back. Mom said Walker would be late anyway. There were problems at the office. Some days he worked until midnight, I knew. So I went.

"Hello, stranger," Kirstie said when she saw me.

"Hey," I said. "Can you get some time off?"

She rolled her eyes. "Some people never learn." She sort of sang it, gesturing toward her mob of marks, all just dying for an opportunity to lay down a buck for a chance at a two-dollar stuffed animal. "Come back later."

"I'm not sure I can." I touched the beeper in my pocket. "I need to get home soon."

"There you go again."

"What?"

"Checking that beeper." She collected a dollar from a kid, then strolled over to try and bait some guys my age into playing. I watched how she worked them, making eye contact and showing off her body, same as she'd done with me that first day. Same as she was doing now. Only when she threatened to move away did they pay. She started the game with a ring of the bell. She came back to me. "Still here?"

"Should I leave?"

"I want you to stay. It doesn't do any good, checking your beeper every two minutes to make sure it's working."

"I don't—"

"Don't you?" She glanced at my pocket. My hand was on it, and I jerked it away. "You've been doing it the past week. At first I thought it was a nervous tic, maybe."

"Maybe it is."

"I know what it's like, you know?"

"What what's like?"

"Hating to go home, but being afraid what will happen if you don't. Not knowing whether to be loyal to someone else, or to yourself."

"Look, can't we just—"

"Drop it? Sure." The game ended again, and again she walked away.

She spent longer with the two guys this time. When she returned I said, "You don't know anything."

"Is it your father?"

"No." Too quickly. "Don't have one of those."

"Stepdad, then?"

I reached for the beeper, then stopped my hand.

"Look, it's no big deal. He doesn't beat me up or anything."

"What does he do?"

"He doesn't do anything to me!"

"What does he do, Michael?"

"He doesn't do anything to me," I repeated. I was lying, and she knew it. We both did.

"I know you can get beat up from the inside, Michael. Get beat up without anyone laying a hand on you."

She laid her hand on me then, fingers touching mine. I felt myself nod. Her hand was cool, soft, like I remembered my mother's hand on my forehead when I had a fever long ago.

"He beats up my mother," I said. "He beats her, and I have to watch it."

It seemed like all the music went silent a moment, probably in my head. I figured she'd walk away, that she'd hate me. *I* hated me, weakling that I was, watching, powerless. And what I really hated was, I *wanted* to be there at the carnival with Kirstie, instead of home doing something about it.

She kept touching my fingers. Her hand, softer than I remembered, stayed there.

"It's hard . . . watching. Isn't it?"

I felt something like a sob, curling in my throat. But I would not cry. I choked out, "Look . . . why don't you go hit on one of those guys? I need to go."

Her eyes went sort of steely then, and she walked off. I stayed, watching her fawn over the guys. One of them finally won a round. I couldn't hear what he said to her, but he gestured toward me, and Kirstie shook her head.

When she came back my way, I said, "What was he saying?"

"What do you care?"

"Look, I'm sorry. I'm going nuts, okay? That's no excuse, but I am."

"Then why don't you just stop worrying about it?"

"Yeah, right. I can just stop." I slapped the side of my head. "Wow, how about that? I stopped worrying. Boy, that was a great idea!"

Kirstie looked at me. "Are you done?"

"I guess."

"Does worrying make her leave the asshole? Does it even make her get beat up less?"

I thought about that day in the dining room. I'd probably made things worse.

"Michael, sometimes you have to help yourself because that's the only one you can help."

Maybe it was because of what she'd said, or maybe it was because it was what I wanted to do anyway. But I stayed late that night.

• • •

The next day, Mom was wearing a turtleneck in eighty-degree weather. I couldn't say I was surprised.

"You didn't beep me," I said.

She spent a while trying to convince me that the turtleneck was because it was cold in the house. But finally she said, "It was nothing. It was over before it started. I didn't want—"

I nodded before she could finish and left.

I went outside and started walking. I didn't know where, just away. I should have been home last night. I should have stopped it.

I was running then. It was rush hour on the bridge. A line of cars snaked out to the mainland. My eyes stung from the rainbow haze of gas fumes. I barely noticed the traffic. Cars honked, and swerved to avoid me. One guy gave me the finger. A woman swore in Spanish. I didn't care. I knew where I was going now. I'd find Walker. I'd get him. I wasn't some kid, some ninety-eight-pound weakling who had to take it because there was nothing else to do. It had been a year since I'd confronted Walker physically. I'd gotten bigger since then. He'd just gotten older. I was weak then. Now my anger made me strong. I was a man. I'd finish this.

My sneakers pounded on the bridge. Each step was a metallic thud. The bridge shuddered with each passing car. I looked at Biscayne Bay below and wondered how it would be, to dive, to swim for it. Would I die when I hit the bay? Or would I turn superhuman, fly through the air, then cut through water like a torpedo? I kept running. I'd hated doing nothing. Now I was doing something.

• • •

Hurry up, and wait.

I'd stood by Walker's car for more than an hour by

his dashboard clock. It was seven thirty, and the parking garage security guard eyed me when he passed the second time.

"I'm waiting for my stepfather," I explained. "Mr. Monroe?"

"Monroe. . . ." The security guard was an older guy, and after a second he gave me a knowing smile. "Ah, your mother's the . . ."

The secretary. The gold digger.

"She used to work here, right? Pretty blond girl." He nodded. "How's she doing?"

She's been better.

"Fine. Walker's supposed to be driving me to . . . track team practice." I gestured toward my clothes. "Guess he forgot."

"Go up to his office, maybe. He sometimes stays until nine or ten."

I shook my head. I wanted the element of surprise. To go up, I'd have to call and be let in. "It's after hours. I don't think he'd answer the phone to get me into the building."

"I can let you in the lobby." The guy patted the keys in his pocket.

I nodded and followed him into the elevator. The place was almost empty, and the night air was cold against my damp T-shirt and hair. We reached the front

156

door, and he let me in.

The lobby was empty. I waited for another elevator, wondering what I'd find when I reached the top. The bell rang, and two lawyer-type guys got out.

"I hated having to tell him," said one. "He hired *me*. I was so impressed with him then. He built this firm from the ground up—they say he comes from nothing too."

"Hey, it ain't over 'til it's over." The second guy loosened his tie. "Maybe the old man will shape up. But there's no room here for deadwood."

The elevator door closed in front of me.

I rode to the twenty-fifth floor, which was entirely devoted to the offices of Monroe, Reyes, Friedman, Geerling, and Nicholson. I remembered the firm name had changed last year, when they'd merged with that guy Reyes' office. We'd heard an earful about that.

The receptionist there was gone too, so I sat on the steps that went up to the rest of the firm's offices, in the penthouse. I waited. It was dark and getting darker, but I curled up on the hard step, listening for sounds. I had to. If Walker decided to take the elevator from the top floor, I could miss him. I didn't intend to miss him.

I heard the AC go off. It began to get warm. I stayed there. Half an hour. An hour.

Finally I heard shoes on the steps above me. I looked up. It was Walker.

I don't think he saw me there in the shadows. He carried a briefcase, and his tie was off, his shirt rumpled. He looked tired. I listened to his footsteps on the spiral staircase. When he'd almost reached bottom, I made my move. I stood, grabbed him, and threw him against the wall.

"You and I are going to have it out right now!"

He looked dazed at first, not seeming to understand who I was. I pulled him back, then slammed him against the wall again, so hard my hands vibrated and hurt from the impact.

A second passed.

He said, "Have what out?"

His voice was strangled.

"You know what!" I let go of him. He stumbled on the stairway, almost falling. I would have let him, but he caught himself, so I took hold of his collar again. He was heavy, but I shook him. "What you do to her, you asshole! What you're doing. I'm not putting up with it anymore. Hit her again, and I'll kick your ass!"

I tightened my grip. He wasn't fighting back. Why hadn't I seen it before? He was old. He was old, and I was strong. There was nothing he could do to me. I was in charge.

I looked into his eyes, at the crow's feet around them. I loosened my grip just a little.

He said, "Why don't you do it now?"

"What?"

"You want to beat the hell out of me? Do it. I won't even put up a fight."

I stared at him. I realized then that I was only holding him because he was letting me.

"Really," he said. "It's the quickest way I can think of to get rid of you. Building security will call the cops. They'll stick you in juvenile with a bunch of guys just waiting for a piece of your pretty, white ass."

He slipped out of my grip and stood straight.

"You wouldn't do that," I said. "I'd tell them. I'd tell them what you do. Everyone would know."

"Think they'd believe you? You think anyone would believe you over me? I'm a respected attorney. You—you're a punk."

I stared.

"You still going to hit me?" He smiled. "Don't let me stop you, tough guy."

When I didn't move, he said, "Didn't think so."

His fist was like a blade to my stomach. I fell into black redness. Then he was gone.

• • •

The next day I took Mom's beeper with a sort of awful relief. Relief because I knew nothing would happen. Walker's hang time always extended at least twenty-four hours. He'd hit something in the past day, so she was safe. But awful because it was a lie. She wouldn't beep me if something happened. I couldn't do anything anyway. I was weak. I hated being weak almost as much as I hated Walker.

• • •

I brought Karpe with me to the fair that night. "Do you mind?" I asked Kirstie.

"Nah—he's a sweet guy."

I shrugged. It was a weird thing to say.

"I'll get him a date," Kirstie said. "It'll be fun."

The date turned out to be Ni-Jin, the contortionist. We sat at tables by the food tent, except Ni-Jin (whose real name, it turned out, was Tiffany), who sat on the ground in the lotus position, smoking a cigarette, while Karpe, obviously starstruck, quizzed her about her career.

"Did you always want to be in show biz?" he asked. "How long have you done this? Is it hard? What's your favorite position? I mean . . . you know what I mean."

And Ni-Jin explained that her family were circus performers for generations. She'd hoped for Ringling Brothers, "but those assholes don't know a great act when they see one."

"Maybe Cirque du Soleil," Karpe suggested.

The girl brightened. "I was thinking about that, too. Hey, I'll show you something cool."

"What?"

"Get me another cigarette first."

"You shouldn't smoke," Karpe said. "My dad's an oncologist, a cancer doctor. If you saw the photos I've seen of people's lungs after they've smoked for years, you'd never do it."

I nudged him. "Yeah, Karpe, that's a turn-on. Talk about diseased lungs on a date."

"'S okay." Tiffany crushed out her cigarette, then lifted first one leg, then the other over her head. While Karpe's eyes popped, she said, "My dad says that too. He worries about me, says it'll stunt my growth."

She was maybe four foot nine. She crossed her legs behind her neck. Gross. I looked away.

"How about you?" I asked Kirstie a second later. "Anyone worrying about you?"

She shook her head. "No one but me cares whether I live or die."

"I care." I leaned to kiss her.

"Ouch!"

We looked over. Tiffany had Karpe on the floor now. She held his leg, trying to bring it over his head.

"Looks like they're having fun," Kirstie said. "What if we went someplace else?"

I nodded. "I know the perfect place."

THIS YEAR

"Are you okay?" Angela asks in the parking lot of the Miami-Dade Detention Center.

"Fine." I try not to look at the barbed wire. I'm thinking, instead, that in a few minutes maybe I'll have my answer. Maybe my mother will tell me what to do.

"Are you sure you're okay?" Angela says, minutes later. We've gone through the metal detector and a guard is frisking me, even under my clothes.

"Hey, watch it, buddy!"

The guard doesn't stop. "You at the jail now."

"Yes, I'm sure," I tell Angela. Though I don't know exactly what I'm saying I'm sure about. I think about leaving. All I have to do is turn around. No one made me come here, and no one will ever make me come back.

But I know I can't go on like this anymore, with this falling feeling, like I stepped off a moving skyride and there's nowhere to go but down or darkness.

"Yeah, I'm sure," I tell Angela.

"You're done." The guard brings us to the door, unlocks it, then opens it. The door leads to a hallway with another locked door at the end.

"I can't believe she's here," I tell Angela. "I mean, it smells." It smells like nothing I've ever smelled before, sweet sourness, like years of sweat.

The first door clangs shut. The sound is hard and permanent. The guard unlocks first one lock, then the other, on the second door. He brings us into another room, which is full of people, mostly women, but there are even little kids and a baby being carried by an old lady. So many people it's almost hard to breathe. They're all on phones, talking to people on the other side of a piece of thick, dirty plastic. Angela grabs my wrist, and we take an empty chair in front of the window. She keeps touching my hand after we sit.

I nod toward the wall phone. "God, there are really phones," I say. "Like on TV. I thought maybe I could just . . . talk to her."

The words are still in the stinking air when Mom walks in.

She has on a blue jumpsuit and stares straight ahead. She's lost weight, even though she was always thin. Now she looks barely real. Her hair is shoulder length and brownish. The guard turns her toward us, directing her to a chair. That's when her eyes meet mine.

Her eyes are the same, but she doesn't blink. She doesn't flinch. She doesn't recognize. I feel myself reach for her, but I know it's dumb, so I sit on my hand.

"Can she see us?" I ask Angela. I'm thinking maybe it's a two-way mirror or something because she doesn't look at me. But on the other side of the glass, a woman prisoner reaches out to the baby, so I know they can see.

Angela wipes the wall phone on her skirt, then hands it to me. The guard pushes my mother into her chair, not roughly, but like a parent with a little kid. He hands my mother the phone.

She is so thin. When she starts to speak, I can't hear. Everyone's shouting around me. I yell, "I can't hear you!"

"Please go," her whispery voice says in my ear. "Please, Michael. There's nothing you can do here."

"I can't leave," I shout. But part of me is thinking, *Why not?*

"You have to."

"I can't do this anymore. It's not fair. I can't stand—"

"Go! Don't you see? This . . ." She gestures around her. "This is what I want, what I deserve. I was a bad mother. I failed you. This is the only way I can make it up to you . . . please, Michael. I don't want this. I don't want them even to know you were there when it happened. I don't want . . ."

Beside me, the baby is screaming. I look around, trying to see if anyone else heard my mother's words. *I don't want them to know you were there when it happened.* No one did, and I don't know whether I've dodged a bullet. Part of me wants to repeat the words loud and long so Angela and everyone can hear. To tell the truth: I was there when Walker died.

"I want to tell them," I say into the phone. "This was a bad idea. I can't pretend anymore."

"Please go," she says again. "Please let me do this for you."

"But—"

She hangs up the phone. I see her speak to the guard, then rise. She walks ahead of him to the door. He unlocks it. Then she's gone.

Angela stares at me, and I want to tell her, but I still can't form the words.

"She told me to leave," I say.

"And will you?"

"No."

LAST YEAR

"That's where I threw my first touchdown pass," I told Kirstie later that night. "First time I played quarterback."

I pointed. We were at the football field at the park near the fairgrounds. It was empty except for Kirstie and me. Football season was long over. It was three A.M., and Kirstie lay in my arms in the cool grass. I'd decided this was going to be our night, the night I made my move with her. It had been a week since I met her, but I felt like I'd known her a hundred years. In some ways, maybe I had. So sleeping with her seemed inevitable. I wanted sleeping with her to be enough.

"How old were you?" she asked.

"Twelve. I begged my mom to let me play—my friend Tristan already did. But she was afraid I'd get hurt. She always protected me. Even when she finally gave in, I think she told Coach Fernandez not to play me, because he didn't put me in until there were about thirty seconds left."

"Lots of pressure for a kid."

"The score was 3-10, them, and the other side had possession, so our defense was in. Then they fumbled. I was already taking off my pads, and Coach put me in. I couldn't believe it."

Just telling Kirstie about it, I could feel the roughness of the ball against my hands. The grass and dirt beneath me smelled the same as that day, and the scent brought memories like some smells do.

I sat up, pointing. "We're lined up on the twenty. There's time for two plays, no more. The first, running, we gain maybe two yards. With nine seconds left, I knew I'd have to pass.

"But when we start again, I freeze. I'd thrown, like, a million passes in my head, memorized the passing tree like it was the multiplication table. But now this big kid's bearing down on me, and I can't move, can't throw. I'm thinking about going home and having my mom make me a bowl of chicken-and-stars soup and telling her she was right.

"Then, the ball's flying away over everyone's head. I still don't remember throwing it, but then everyone's screaming, crushing into me." I looked at Kirstie. "It was like nothing bad ever happened, and I knew the only thing I wanted to do—ever—was play ball."

I was grinning. I still heard the cheers.

"Do you still play?" she asked.

"N-no . . . I . . ."

"Quit?"

I nodded, though she couldn't see me in the dark.

Still, she said, "Stupid."

"I didn't have a choice. My mother—"

"You always have a choice."

"Look, can we just . . . ?" *Can we just make out? Can we just not talk about this?* I wanted to say. But I couldn't, so I changed the subject. "You never told me about your family. I don't know anything about you before here."

"Maybe there isn't anything before here." She tilted her head back, looking at the sky. "Maybe I was born here. Sometimes I feel like I was."

"But you weren't."

"No. No, I wasn't."

I sensed she was going to say more, so I waited.

We sat there until I thought maybe I was wrong. I started thinking maybe I should go home. I was okay as long as it was noisy with the lights and music and people. But when it got quiet, I'd start thinking about home.

Finally, I began to stand, but she reached out, tugged on my arm. When I looked at her, she said, "You want to know about me?"

"You don't have to," I said, backing off.

"You want to know?"

I nodded and sat back down. The ground was cold and a little wet. I started to pull her closer again, but she was busy, fumbling with the leather bracelets she wore. She unsnapped one, then held up her arm, turning it over so I could see it in the moonlight.

"That's me," she said.

I didn't see what she meant at first. Then I saw the mottled skin and faded reddish scars on her wrist. She undid the second bracelet so I could see that it matched.

"Who did it to you?" I said, though I knew.

"I did. I did it the year my mother died."

"Did it hurt?" I reached to take her arm. She pulled away at first, then she let me grasp and hold it. I felt the little ridges where the scars were, criss-crossing with the blue hills of her veins. "I mean . . . when you did it?"

"I wasn't thinking about whether it hurt at the time. But later—after they found me—later it hurt."

"Does it still?"

"No. Scars don't hurt. They're just . . . there."

"Why'd you do it?"

She shrugged. "Didn't want to be alive anymore."

"But, I mean—"

"Because I'd failed. I wasn't supposed to fail. It's not how I was raised."

I looked closer at her arm. "What'd you fail at, Kirstie?"

She pulled her arm away and stood, walked closer to the goalpost.

"When I was six, my father was vice president of the bank in town. He went to New York for a business trip and brought me back this parasol from Chinatown—a paper one, like they put in a drink, only life-size. I loved it. I carried it so much, the kids in the neighborhood used to make fun of me. But I was so proud, I didn't care. My dad had bought it.

"Then, a month later, this man came over to visit—the *president* of the bank, I guess. He had a little girl, and I was supposed to play with her. But she scared my cat and broke my dolls, and when they were on the way out, she saw my parasol and said, 'Daddy, I want it.'

"My father said, 'I'm sure Kirsten would be happy to let you have it,' all the time giving me a look that wouldn't let me refuse. And, next thing I knew, that mean little girl was leaving with my Chinese parasol.

"I started to cry, watching them go. And my father slapped me and said, 'Think of someone else for a change.' He didn't offer to buy me a new parasol next time he went. I wouldn't have wanted it anyway, because it wouldn't have been mine. Not really."

"What an asshole," I said.

"Yeah, but he was my father. He said I needed to think of others more, and I bought it." She looked over her shoulder at me. "How long was that touchdown pass anyway?"

"Eleven yards," I said.

"That's really good for a little kid."

I nodded. If I concentrated, I could still see the ball, spiraling over and over, like a nautilus shell.

"Really, really good."

I said, "The thing with the parasol—where was your mother when it happened?"

Kirstie shrugged. "Could have been in the kitchen, hand-washing the dishes. Could have been out back, composting the strawberries to feed the roses. Or she could have been in bed, crying."

"Crying?"

"My mother had . . . mood swings. One day she'd be great—baking five hundred sugar cookies for kids to decorate at the Police Benevolent Association Christmas party. The next day she'd be on the kitchen floor, crying, because the meat loaf didn't turn out right. Or she'd go weeks without brushing her hair."

"Did someone take care of her?" I asked.

"I took care of her. My father said we couldn't tell anyone. They'd use it to hurt us, use it to hurt *him*. My sister and I, we were already hurting. So he took her to this doctor out of town."

She crossed her arms over her chest.

"But the doctor couldn't get her medication right. It's like when you're trying to tune an old radio. You go one way and get country-western, the other way and get shock talk—when really, you're trying to land on the Top 40 station. That's how it was, first one extreme, then the other, and I had to stand over her to make sure she took her meds—then watch them not work. By the time I was eight, I was doing all the cooking, most of the cleaning, helping my little sister, Erica, with her homework, you name it. I had no friends, my grades were for shit, and every once in a while my mother had an episode when she'd think the house was on fire and run outside into the night. Or once, she got in the car and drove downtown, then sat perfectly still at a stop sign until the police called Daddy to take her home."

"That must have been tough."

She shrugged. "I always got in trouble when that happened. 'Just don't let anything upset her,' my father said, like that was possible. So I was really careful what I said. I didn't tell her if anyone was sick, stuff like that, even bad stuff on the news. 'You're in control,' he told me."

"Talk about pressure."

"Yeah. Well, when I was fifteen, I gave in to pressure. I met this guy, Clay. He paid attention to me, and he told me I didn't need to sit home with Mom all the time. And I believed him. I fell in love. We started partying together—smoking, having sex. It was amazing how after I took the pills he gave me I could just forget about home. We were together all the time, and for the first time I was thinking about myself. I told myself Erica should handle Mom for a change, but Erica was only eleven. She didn't know all the things I knew. She wasn't me."

Kirstie leaned against the goalpost, burying her head in one hand. In the distance I could hear the swoosh-swoosh of traffic on Eighth Street, but I was listening for Kirstie's voice.

When she didn't speak, I walked toward her.

"You don't have to tell me any more if you don't want," I said. But I wanted her to.

She raised her head. "We don't talk about our pasts here. Everyone has one, and they're all more or less horrible. But I want to tell you, Michael. You're the only person I've ever wanted to tell."

I touched her elbow, then thought better of it and drew away. She continued.

"The day before my sixteenth birthday, I had a fight with Mom. I'd been pretty good that day. At least, I'd done a load of laundry and cleaned up the kitchen a little bit. But later, I was on my way out, and Mom didn't want me to go.

"'Please, Kirsten,' she was begging. 'I just don't know if I can handle it.'

173

"'What's to handle?' I said. 'Just go to bed and lie there. That's all you do anyway.'

"The words just sort of stayed there, like a piece of furniture in the room. I tried to say I was sorry, but it was too late. My mother sighed and said, 'You're right.' And she went to bed.

"My birthday's in February, and that February was one of the coldest I can remember. But we stayed warm, partying, getting trashed. I think I was trying to forget what I'd said to Mom. When I got home, I stumbled up the stairs. It was so dark, I couldn't see anything.

"But the next morning I found her. She was slumped on a bench in the backyard, where our rose garden was. I don't know if she was waiting for me or if she just forgot it was cold and wandered out there."

"Aw, Kirstie, you couldn't—"

"I'll never know if I could've saved her if I'd been home. But a few weeks later, when I was upstairs cleaning out her things, I found about two weeks' worth of pills, stuffed under her mattress." Kirstie's voice caught in her throat. "I hadn't been there to give them to her, so she hadn't taken them."

"You don't know that's what happened." I put my arm around her. "It could have been old pills. You said they didn't work anyway."

"Yeah, I told myself that. And I told myself she might as well be dead, as much as her life was worth. And then I picked up every one of those pills and shoved them under my own mattress. I was going to take them myself, all of them at once. But I didn't because I didn't know what they'd do to me. Like, maybe they wouldn't kill me. Maybe they'd just make me crazy like Mom. When your mom's nuts, you start thinking you might be too, you know? That was a big part of the problem."

She pulled away and showed me her wrists again.

"But instead, I did this. I failed at that, too. My sister found me and called an ambulance. I remember her sitting beside me while she waited for them. I wasn't totally conscious, but I remember her holding my arms, begging me, 'Don't leave. Don't you leave too.'"

Kirstie walked away, over to where we'd been sitting, and picked up the leather bracelets. She started to put them back on.

"At the hospital they put me in, they told me it wasn't my fault. *Everyone* told me that. I had individual therapy, group therapy, role playing—all to tell me I wasn't responsible. I still didn't believe them, but I decided not to think about it. I decided I wanted to live anyway, just not with my family. A few weeks after I came home, the carnival was in town. I went there with Erica, but I ditched her with some friends at the funnel-cake booth.

I told her I was going on the Zipper, but really I went to the circus tent. I found a circus performer who told me how to get a job with them. I lied about my age. I've been here ever since.

"What I like about it here is you never have to apologize. You never have to live with your mistakes for more than a week or so." She played with her bracelet, the one she hadn't put on yet. "And no one needs you for anything more important than work."

"So you never saw your father or sister again?"

She shook her head. "Didn't want to." Then she thought about it. "No, that's not true. I want to see Erica. Some days I'll see a kid who looks like her and I just about fall apart . . . but if I ever went back, she'd probably hate me for leaving."

I walked over and sat beside her. "I bet she wouldn't hate you. I bet she'd be happy to see you back."

Kirstie shrugged. "Doesn't matter. I'm not going back. I couldn't handle it there. I had to get away, or I'd . . ." She looked at her wrists.

I did too. "Kirstie, I . . ." I touched her wrist. "I thought about doing that too. Or something like that anyway. I know how it is."

She didn't ask why, just put her arms around me. She held me there a few minutes, listening to the sounds from the fairgrounds—music and laughter over the trees.

"I hate the real world," she said.

"Yeah. Me too."

"Are you still good at football?"

I nodded.

She pulled away from me, walking toward the shadows where the moon didn't reach. I thought maybe she was leaving, but she came back a moment later, holding an old, squashy-looking football.

"Some kid must have left it here," she said.

"Poor kid."

She walked to me, touched my nose. "Poor kid."

"Nah."

She held up the ball. "I want to see you throw a pass."

I started to shake my head no, but she shoved it into my hands, and suddenly, I did want to throw it, for old time's sake. Even if the ball was rotting and old. I gestured for her to run out, and she did. I waited until she was far away, near the goal line, before I made the pass, predicting where she'd be when it dropped. It didn't go as far as a good ball, but she ran up and caught it.

She started running the other way. "She intercepts!"

I pursued her, slowly at first, to give her a chance to get ahead. But then in earnest. I caught her on what would have been the fifty-yard line. I tackled her, kissing her. She let me this time. Then she kissed me back. Her kiss was a powerful drug that made me forget about goal-posts and the scars on her wrists and what I was going to say—anything but my hands on her body, her warmth against the cool night. I started unbuttoning her jeans.

She pulled away.

"Come with me," she said.

"Sure. Where? I mean . . . wherever you want."

I started to stand.

"No," she said, stopping me. "I mean, come *with* me. When I go, *we* go."

I realized what she was suggesting and slumped back down.

"You mean, come with you . . . like forever?"

"Nothing's forever. But for now. Yeah. Come with me, Michael."

Her voice was excited for the first time since I'd known her. For an instant, the word *yes* was on my tongue.

"I can't."

"You can. You just won't."

"I can't."

"The same thing will happen, Michael, whether you stay or not. It's not your responsibility. And—not your fault."

She meant at home. I said, "It would be easier if I could believe that."

"But you don't?"

"I don't know what I believe. But I have to stay."

She nodded. "Guess that's why I like you. Most guys, they're just looking for a way to leave."

She sat down again on the grass a second. I wondered if she was mad, but then she took my hand in both of hers.

She didn't move to kiss me again. In the distance I could hear the carnival people even though it was close to three. The lights from their trailers and from Eighth Street kept the stars from showing, so it was almost like daytime. Kirstie guided my fingers to her scarred wrist. I felt the healed ridges and knew she was showing me that healing was possible.

I felt the steady beat of her pulse beneath them.

THIS YEAR

"What will you do now?" Angela asks as we get into her blue Mini in the jail parking lot. She hasn't spoken since we left the visiting room. Or maybe she's spoken but I haven't heard. I'm still thinking about what Mom said, the decision I know I'll need to make soon: Tell the whole truth, or go.

I notice for the first time there's people around, cops and stuff. All I've seen since I left is Mom's face, her face the day it happened. All I can hear is her screams, Walker's falling body.

"What happened to the house?" I ask.

"The house?" But I can tell she knows what I mean, so I wait.

"I'm not sure. Your mother will get it—and everything of his—if she's acquitted. But I'm not sure what they're doing with it while she's on trial."

"Can we go there?"

She doesn't ask me why. She says, "If someone had a key, they could probably get in."

"I can get in."

. . .

"Drive around back," I tell Angela.

"Michael—trespassing."

I'm so beyond caring about trespassing. But I say,

"I'm not breaking in. And we'll only stay a few minutes. I just have to see it. I just have to . . ." *remember.*

Angela looks like she wants to say something else, but drives around. I walk to the garage and punch in a combination on the keypad. 323. Walker and Mom's anniversary. The door rumbles up, and I remember all the times, sitting with Mom, waiting to bolt when I heard it. I feel my armpits get wet under my T-shirt. The sweat is cold in the March wind. I lead Angela through the garage, close the door, and use my key to open the inner door.

Inside feels gray, still. Dead palmetto bugs, legs up, litter the floor like they came out when the house was quiet, then died for lack of food. I picture the floor swarming with them.

"She used to clean so much," I said, "to keep bugs from coming in. It's a big house. It took most of her day just to clean."

"Were you surprised to hear she did it?"

"Huh?" I'm still thinking about the house, but then I realize what Angela means.

"Seeing her today," Angela says, "I understood what you meant. She didn't seem capable of it."

I wonder if she knows the truth, knows I was there and is testing me. I say, "I don't know. Maybe, sometimes, you just don't know what people are capable of.

I mean, if you're just getting beat up, day in, day out, maybe you just . . . snap at some point."

Angela nods. I walk through the kitchen, dining room, living room. At the front door I look back.

"They left the furniture," I say.

"It will be a while. This house will be a hard sell, with its history."

If you didn't know the place well, you'd think it was exactly the same. But I notice right off that my mother's embroidered runner's missing. I start toward the stairs, to my room.

"This is where I slept," I tell Angela. I can tell the room's been gone through, maybe by someone cleaning, maybe by someone looking for clues about where I am. Things like trophies and even my *Sports Illustrated*s are placed differently. I remember the room like I'm seeing a photograph.

"Why are we here, Michael?"

I have to see it. I have to make sense of it. My mother has given me permission to leave, ordered me to, even. I should take it, I know.

"I didn't do anything," I say to Angela. "I studied. I slept. At night, I'd lie here, hearing them. I heard him hurting her, and I didn't do anything."

"You were a kid, Michael. You shouldn't have been in that situation."

"Why didn't I do anything?"

"You were afraid. It's okay to be afraid, Michael."

I walk away from her and crank open the window. I can hear the ocean. And then it seems like all the sounds close up around me and there's silence. I know what comes next, and I can't be there anymore. I bolt for the stairs.

When I reach the bottom, I stop:

Downstairs, the lights blazed yellow. The runner on the hallway table was ripped. Stuff that had been on top of it lay scattered, broken, on the floor.

My body felt cold, then warm. Then I heard the scream.

The cold heat moved me. I ran toward the study.

"Michael! Wait!" Angela's voice sounds like it's at the bottom of the ocean.

I keep going.

There was a full moon the night Walker was killed. That and the lights from downtown should have made it easy to see, even in the dark house.

Easy.

But I couldn't see. I tiptoed into the study, staring straight ahead out the terrace doors, knowing where I was going, but not seeing. I heard footsteps, stopped, then realized they were my own. Heard my breath in my ears, sounding like the inside of my football helmet when I used to play.

The walk seemed long, but it was really only a few feet. I reached the sofa but didn't touch it. I looked out the backlit doors and tried to decide where to go next.

I didn't want to step on him.

I leaned toward the table lamp. My hand brushed something wet, and I recoiled.

"Stop, Michael!"

It was my mother's voice.

"Michael!"

I'm in the study. All the furniture is missing, rugs, everything. But I stare at the spot where I know Walker's body was. Know Walker's body was because I was there. Because I saw it.

Angela, I was there. I . . .

But I can't say it. I can't. Angela touches my shoulder.

"Michael, are you okay?" Her voice comes from somewhere else.

"This is where it was, right? Where it happened?" Even though I know.

"Yes." Angela points to the fireplace. I see her pointing, her mouth moving.

"Sometimes, I can still hear it," I say.

What? she mouths. *Hear what?*

"Her screaming," I say. *And Walker's body, hitting the ground.*

Sometimes at night, and even during the day when there's a lot going on, the noise around me closes up and goes away and I hear it. The impact.

I hear it now, Walker's body hitting the floor, then her scream. Since I've been back in Miami, I hear it more and more. I try to make myself think about something else, but the sound is stuck in my ears like guitar feedback. The impact of his death.

"I wanted him to die," I say.

"But that's normal. He beat your mother. He emotionally tortured you. He—"

I know it's not normal, but I let myself believe her words, believe that what my mother is saying is right, and I say, "Let's get out of here."

•   •   •

And then we're back in her car again, driving on Rickenbacker, seeing the water on both sides like it's going to engulf us and swallow up the road. Angela's silent, and so am I. But I hear it still. Finally, I reach over and turn on the radio. It's the top of the hour, so I fiddle with the dial until I find a news station.

Jury selection completed in the Lisa Monroe murder trial . . . twelve jurors and four alternates . . . opening arguments beginning tomorrow . . .

"That means . . . ?"

"They have a jury," she says. "Tomorrow the lawyers

will start their opening arguments, telling their side of the story."

"Will my mother be there?"

"Yes, they bring the accused to trial to watch. It's part of the Constitution, and it humanizes her to the jury. She won't say anything, though. First the lawyers make their opening arguments. Then the state attorney—the other side—presents their evidence."

"Why do they go first?"

"They have the burden of proof. They go first because if the state doesn't prove what it needs to, the trial stops."

"And will that happen?"

She shakes her head. "She confessed. They'll present that confession, the physical evidence of the crime, like blood-spatter patterns, the fingerprints. It should take a week or so. Then her lawyers will present their evidence, their defense."

"Will she have to talk . . . I mean, testify?"

"She *is* their evidence." Angela turns off Rickenbacker onto the mainland.

"Do you think she's guilty?" I ask.

"I think she's afraid. I think she thought he'd kill her."

"You think that because of what I said?"

Angela nods. We sit in silence.

Finally I say, "Tell me the truth—do you think she'll

be convicted if I don't speak up?"

Angela turns on her signal and changes lanes before saying, "I think she may be convicted either way, Michael. Seeing her today, it seemed like she wants to be convicted."

In my ears, I hear the impact again and again.

LAST YEAR

The fair would be there another week, no more. It was in town nineteen days total—started on a Wednesday and ended on a Sunday. Next Sunday. The following day they'd take down the games and the circus tent, dismantle the Tilt-a-Whirl and the double Ferris wheel, pack up the petting zoo, and head for their next stop, leaving the fairgrounds a wasteland of trodden-down grass and broken pavement.

"You can make good money helping with teardown," Cricket told me.

I shook my head. "It's a school day."

But it wasn't school. I'd become barely a shadow at school anyway. It was that I was wondering whether I could do it. To see this place without the lights, the music, and more important, without the people. And to know that they were someplace else, without me.

And the thought nagged at me that Kirstie was right. I didn't need to stay. There was nothing I could do— Walker had proven that.

Since that day at the football field, Kirstie and I hadn't discussed her leaving. But I felt the truth between us like a force field. We spent hours just walking around the fairgrounds talking or doing stuff with her friends after hours (Karpe sometimes tagged along, and he said he was becoming more limber). But she never took me behind the scenes, where she called home. I didn't ask her to either. It wasn't that I was scared of sleeping with her. I wasn't. But maybe I was scared that if I became too much a part of her world, I wouldn't be able to go back to my own.

The night that Cricket asked me about teardown, I tried to talk to her. "Kirstie, about what we were discussing. About staying. . . ."

She put her finger to my lips.

"Shh. Let's just enjoy it while we can."

• • •

At school, Miss Hamasaki called me up to her desk.

"Michael Daye, I need to speak to you."

It was Thursday, the day of Alex Ramos's party, and more people were talking about it than thinking about English. Still, Miss Hamasaki noticed when I fell asleep during a pop quiz and she'd had to peel my blank paper out from under me.

"I'm sorry about the quiz," I said. "It won't happen again."

"It's not that—although Mrs. Corman said you were a solid B student in her class last year, which surprised me quite a bit. But your grades aren't specifically what I'm concerned about."

Danger! Danger was strobing like an ambulance

light across the green-painted classroom walls. I remembered Walker's words, *You think anyone would believe you over me?*, his cool handling of the social worker who'd shown up that time. Then, his anger.

I said, "Then there's nothing to worry about. I'm fine."

"Is that true, Michael? Because falling grades can sometimes indicate . . ."

She was young, a first-year teacher, probably only a year or two older than Kirstie. She didn't know the old Michael Daye, didn't know me from any stoner who used the school as a base of operations. I could use that.

I made sure to meet her eyes. That was one thing I'd learned from Walker: Meet their eyes, especially when you're lying.

"Old Lady Corman . . ." I finger-combed my hair and lowered my eyes, sort of sleepy, sort of stoned. "She was hot for me. That's why she gave me that *B*." I licked my upper lip real slow. "Do you want to give me a *B?*"

She broke eye contact with a disgusted expression. "Look," she said, gathering the papers on her desk and banging them into a neat pile. "You need to quit sleeping in class and hand in some better papers quick, or you're going to flunk."

"I'll remember that," I said, amazed, sort of, that I could take the idea of failing English so calmly. Last year I'd been upset by that *B*.

I headed for the cafeteria, where I handed Karpe both my sandwiches. I spent the rest of the hour with my head on the table, pretending to sleep.

But really, the noise around me invaded my ears, the vibrations from the feet on the floor and the conversations making the table sound like the inside of a seashell.

•   •   •

I skipped sixth and seventh periods to get to the fair early. There'd been a time when I'd never have skipped, when I'd have been too scared of being caught. Now it was easy.

"Can you get the night off?" I asked Kirstie when I got there. I'd decided to go to Alex's party, like Tristan wanted, but I wanted Kirstie there too. She wore a leather top with buttons down the front. The bottom button was open, and I could see the swell of the bottom of her breasts.

"Thursday night? Not likely."

I looked around. It was barely three, and already the place was beginning to fill up. Teenagers from nearby high schools and little kids, dragging parents in business clothes.

"Please," I said to Kirstie. "Please go with me."

"Sucks being you, doesn't it?"

"You're beautiful," I said.

"Flattery will get you nowhere." But she was smiling a little.

"*You were meant for me.*" I sang it to her. "*And I was meant for you.*"

"You're such a screw-up," she said, laughing. "I guess it wouldn't be hard to find someone to fill in for me."

"Thank you."

"Give me a couple hours, okay?"

My next-biggest problem was Karpe. We'd made plans to go to the fair together, Karpe in hopes of hooking up with Ni-Jin.

I called from a pay phone. I considered lying, but I'd lied so much lately to so many people that I decided to tell the truth for a change.

"I'm not going to the fair tonight," I said when he answered.

"What's wrong?"

"Nothing. I'm just . . . there's this party . . ."

I figured he'd make some comment about my friends, or maybe ask if he could come along. I'd almost have taken him. But he just said, "Okay, maybe some other night."

"Yeah. Tomorrow. I promise."

After getting the address from Tris, I called Mom (they were going out; it was their anniversary). Then I looked for Cricket to see if anyone needed me to work a few hours.

He found some friends who wanted help with their hot dog stand.

"You know, I could talk Mr. Corbett into giving you a real job," Cricket said on his way to the trailer. "That's who gave me my start—Mr. Corbett himself."

I knew the carnival was run by the Corbett Amusements company. The name was on all the programs and garbage cans, even the doors of the johns.

"How did that happen?" I knew I was getting dangerously close to asking the questions you didn't ask, the stuff Kirstie said was on a need-to-know basis.

"I ran away from the group home I was in. Some of the bigger boys was messing with me. So I go to Route 66 and start hitching. I was fourteen and looked younger, and no one wanted to pick up a runaway. Then a truck stopped. The side said *Corbett's Amusements*."

We reached the hot dog trailer. There was a sign on the back that said, *Jesus is the Head of this Operation*, and all these little kids were running around, trying to help a couple who were passing a screaming infant back and forth.

"Shouldn't those kids be in school somewhere?" I asked Cricket.

"They go to school. It's, like, a special carnival school.

They never need nothing more."

He caught the guy's eye and gestured like, *Here he is*.

"So," Cricket said, "Mr. Dale Corbett's driving. He asks where I'm going, and I say I don't care. But by the time we reach the state line, I knew where I was going."

"What state was that?"

Cricket's face darkened. "I don't want to tell you that."

"Sorry." It was weird how here, where everyone had secrets, I felt more comfortable than at school, where it was only me. I could tell anyone here about the problems at home, but I didn't *need* to. Somehow just having the option was enough. Maybe that was what it was all about—options. Home with Walker, I didn't have any. Here, I did. I looked up at the hot dog stand, then back to see Cricket watching me.

"Anyway," Cricket said, "Mr. C. hired me, and I bet he'd hire you. He could pay you under the table, like."

"I don't think so," I said. "Thanks, though. It's just . . . my family."

"Oh, you got one of those. I just thought maybe you were looking to bail. And you have a knack for the carny business."

The hot dog guy finished with his customer and waved us in. "Thanks God you here." He gestured toward the woman. "Now Anna, she can go take care of little Roberto." He put out his hand to Cricket. "Thank you, my friend."

"No biggie," Cricket said. "We all help each other, right?"

"Right."

The woman—the hot dog guy's wife—was still standing there, sort of bouncing the baby. She walked up close to me and held the baby level with my eyes. He stopped crying and stared at me.

"He likes you," she said, smiling.

I put a hand out, touched the baby's soft little feet. "You got some family here, kid."

"We all family here," the hot dog guy said. "All family."

THIS YEAR

"Is it you? The truth."

Cricket's waiting for me when I return to my trailer.

"What are you talking about?" I say. "Look, it's two o'clock. I need to set up. I don't have time for—"

"Don't shit me, man. It's important. You know what I'm talking about." He shoves a paper, the *Herald* photograph in my face again. "Is this you . . . Michael?"

"Where did you get that? What are they, giving them out at the gate now?"

"Some guy out there's showing it to everyone. I think he's a reporter. There were some cops here too."

"The cops aren't looking for me."

"Maybe not. But you can't stay here. You're under-age, and now everyone knows it. You could get us in hot water."

"That's just great. Just turn me in the second things get tough. That's just—"

I stop. I look at Cricket. He's holding out my duffel bag. I haven't seen it since I unpacked last year, and I know I'm being unfair. This is what I signed up for—no obligations on either side. Besides, maybe this is just pushing me to do what I know I have to.

"I'm sorry, Robert."

I take the duffel from him. "The name's Michael. Michael Daye."

He nods and reaches a hand into his pocket and takes out a wad of money. He starts to hand it to me.

"You don't have to."

He shoves the bills into my jacket pocket.

"We were friends, Mike. You'll come back, maybe next year when you're really eighteen, when all this is over."

I nod. But I know I won't be back. "I better get out of here."

I head out to the exit, to the bus stop. The whole way, I can feel Cricket's wad of bills in my pocket. It's big enough that even if it's mostly ones, added to what I already have, I'd have enough to take me far, far away, someplace else I can escape.

But I know I only need a dollar and change to go where I need to go.

LAST YEAR

"Your friend lives here?" Kirstie asked when the bus dropped us off way down Sunset Drive, almost a mile from the address Tristan had given me.

"No. He lives in Coral Gables, near where I live. Just, sometimes people like to have parties where there's no neighbors to complain."

"Playing at being grown-ups."

She was right. My friends at school were little kids compared to people I'd met at the fair. And I was hovering somewhere in between. I thought about all that while we stumbled over the cracked pavement of the old road. Should have brought a flashlight. Every few minutes a car went by, probably one of my friends for the party. But none stopped.

"What are you thinking about?" Kirstie asked, after we jumped out of the way of the third SUV in a row.

"I'm thinking about next week, when you leave."

"What are you thinking about it?"

"I'm thinking I don't want you to."

"Maybe don't think about it then."

She stopped walking and pulled me close to her, kissed me. But she didn't ask me again to stay.

"Is that what you do when something bothers you? You don't think about it?"

"It's better than checking your beeper when it's too late anyway."

We kept walking, Kirstie's words hanging from the bottoms of the ficus and poinciana trees that made a canopy over the road. And soon we were in the driveway.

I saw Tristan, sitting on the doorstep, drinking a beer from a red plastic cup, and I thought that next week that would be me, too.

Earlier, when I'd called Tris for the address, he'd said, "You're really coming?"

"It's just a party," I had answered. "I'm bringing someone, okay?"

"Not that loser, Julian Karpe."

"No." Though I'd had a flash—Karpe and his father eating ravioli out of the can for dinner. "No, it's a girl."

"Ah, so there's a girl involved. You sure you want to do that? Tedder and Vanessa broke up. Or rather, Tedder told all his friends he did it with Vanessa, and she told him to screw off. But she'll probably still be at the party. Everyone will be there."

"Yeah, well, I'm bringing this girl." It seemed like forever ago that girls at school had meant anything to me.

"Bring the girl, Mike. Just show, okay?" And he'd sounded so happy I'd felt bad all over. Maybe I'd misjudged him. Maybe he'd have been fine if I'd told him everything, but it was the uncertainty. That's why I couldn't talk to him. That's what Walker had done—made me uncertain.

But now I hung outside the group, not sure what to do, still not ready.

Kirstie took the first step for me.

"Hey," she said, releasing my hand. "You must be one of Michael's friends."

Tris's beer sloshed out of its cup. "Best friend up to a couple weeks ago. Um . . . you must be Mike's girl."

"I'm Kirstie."

She said this while I was still fumbling for their names, then turned to me. "Where's Julian?"

"He, er, doesn't usually go to these things."

Kirstie raised an eyebrow at that. By then Tris had recovered his voice enough to introduce himself, sort of checking Kirstie out, and not in a good way.

And then Tedder Dutton was filling the doorway.

"Hey, Daye, you made it." He looked both of us up and down. Behind him Tris was mouthing *Hottie* at me. "And you brought someone." He was roasted, leaning against the doorway, trying to look cool, but obviously holding on for balance.

Kirstie introduced herself, then said, "So what's there to do around here?"

Tedder laughed. "Why don't you show your girlfriend where the beer is."

"Oh, beer I can get. I was hoping there'd be something to *do*."

"Maybe we can think of something," Tedder said, eyeing her up and down.

"There's a band out back," I told Kirstie.

Kirstie returned Tedder's look, then followed me through the house.

Inside was pretty much a Xerox copy of every party I'd ever been to. I probably could have navigated it blindfolded, using only my sense of smell and sound.

"To the left," I told Kirstie, "we have geeks playing Quarters. And to the right, we have burnouts smoking weed."

I stopped. I knew a lot of the carnival people did drugs, and not just pot. I knew she'd done them in school. As we traveled through the room, I noticed people stopping whatever they were doing to turn and stare at us.

I said, "And in the center, we have a bunch of guys, looking like they've never seen a woman before."

"Well, they've never seen me before." We stepped out onto the patio. It felt cooler than it had on the road, and I moved closer to Kirstie. The band was playing too loudly for us to talk without shouting, and some more guys were playing Quarters. They, too, stopped to stare at us.

"Why the big tour back there?" she said—shouted—at me.

"I dunno." I took her hand and moved her across the patio, behind the speakers where it wasn't as loud. "Guess they just seemed different than the people you hang with."

"Not a freak show?"

I winced, remembering my comment. Things had changed so much since then. "A different kind of freak show." When she kept looking at me, I said, "Do you think, back when there *were* freak shows, the freaks would look out into the audience and think, 'How strange'?"

"I bet. Some states made laws against displaying human oddities. They said it was to keep these 'unfortunates' from being taken advantage of."

"Makes sense."

"Sort of. But every time they made a law, freaks came out to protest."

"Why?"

"They said they needed to make a living. But I don't think that was the whole reason."

I watched as, to the right, someone sunk a quarter and made the already-trashed guy to his left take a drink.

"Why then?" I said.

"People who made those laws, they wanted to act like nothing was wrong with those freaks, like they were the same as everyone else. But if you've got an eye in the middle of your forehead, you *know* you're not just folks. At least in the carnival you can be with other people like you."

I nodded, thinking about how much easier it was being with people in the carnival who didn't all expect me to be a certain way, to follow their rules. I said, "And show that they were proud too."

"Exactly. But you didn't have to explain your friends to me. Back home I had the exact same kind of friends."

That's when I felt a hard hand on my shoulder. I turned. Tedder.

"Mind if I dance with your date?"

"I don't think so," I said. It was crazy. No one was dancing. People didn't dance at parties like this, at least not until they were really trashed.

But Tedder kept going. "Aw, c'mon, Daye. Your girl-friend here wanted some entertainment. I feel obligated to give it to her. She ought to be more polite."

"I don't think so," I repeated.

A few people had gathered, including Vanessa, who said, "Don't be such an ass, Tedder."

"I didn't ask you," Tedder said. He offered Kirstie his hand.

"I don't think so either," she said. She turned to me. "Maybe we should go, Michael."

I nodded and held out my hand. Kirstie started to take it, then Tedder yanked her away.

"I *asked* you to dance," he growled.

I turned to see him lunge toward Kirstie, his fat hands grabbing at her, and I felt the same way I always felt when Walker beat on Mom. Except I had to take shit from Walker. I didn't have to take it from Tedder Dutton.

"Hey," I said. "Leave her—"

But before I could get the words all the way out, Dutton was headed for the floor. Kirstie had flipped him somehow, his legs flying out from under him, and his ass hit the ground with a thud.

"I have a knife in my pocket," Kirstie said, over him. "You want to make me use it?"

"N-no," Tedder stammered.

"Maybe you didn't hear me before," she said, "but I said I didn't want to dance."

"Okay. Sorry."

She backed off, and he lay there. Monica Correa, who had the hots for Dutton, ran to him. No one else did. They just stood there, staring at Kirstie. I stared too. And the band kept playing and playing, and I knew I could never come back to one of their parties again, and I didn't care.

"Bitch!" Tedder sputtered. "Get your freak girlfriend out of here, Daye."

And Kirstie threw back her head and began to laugh.

• • •

"Do you really have a knife in your pocket?" I asked Kirstie on the way back to the bus stop. I realized I'd almost let myself forget about the problems at home. Almost.

"Sure." She stopped and pulled out a penknife. She flicked open the blade and held it up so it gleamed silver in the moonlight. My arms shivered, feeling like a hundred bees had landed there.

"Why do you have it?"

"The game. Sometimes the balloons get stuck, and I need to cut them off."

"Oh." I relaxed a little.

"That, and for protection."

"You wouldn't . . . I mean, would you really use a knife on someone?" I turned this new fact about her around in my head.

"I never have. I'm not looking for an opportunity like some I know. I mean, back there, I tried to leave. But, yeah, if it's ever me or them, it's gonna be me."

We walked in silence. The road was deserted, dark. No cars were coming anymore, and none were leaving, so the only sound was the scrape-scrape of our shoes against pavement. I thought how different she was from Mom, who always needed someone else to help her.

"But *I* wanted to defend you," I said, knowing as I said it that it was the wrong thing. "I wanted to deck the guy or something. I've been wanting to kick his ass for a while. I tried once, and someone stopped me."

She smiled, though I could only see the outline of it. "I know. I could see in your face how bad you wanted to hit him."

"So why didn't you let me?"

She shrugged. "What would have happened if you'd hit him?"

"There'd have been a big fight."

"And . . . ?"

"I'd have kicked the shit out of him."

"Maybe. Or maybe everyone would have taken his side. He seemed to have a lot of friends there. Maybe they'd have kicked the shit out of you. No. That was my battle. I think it was better to let me fight it."

"With a knife?"

"Carnies are tough people, Michael. You have to be to live this life."

"Why do you want to?" I asked.

"It's all I have now," she said. "I've left everything else."

I slowed my steps, wanting to stay with her longer

and knowing we'd have to split up at the bus stop. I didn't want to.

"Do you . . . ?" I didn't know how to ask what I wanted to ask. "I mean, have there been other guys like me in other places you've been?"

I expected her to maybe get mad at me, like that day on the Ferris wheel when I asked if she'd kissed a lot of guys. But instead, she slowed her steps to match mine.

"No one like you. But, of course, there have been other guys."

"Guys you left and forgot about?" I asked, feeling cruel.

"Not forgot exactly. But, yeah, once you leave the first time, you get used to leaving."

I stopped walking, and so did Kirstie. I could still hear the band at the party if I tried, like the party had gone on without us, the space where we'd been closing up without a patch. But the trees sounded like maracas, and I liked that sound better. I drew Kirstie toward me, putting my fingers on her back, feeling her spine and each little rib. She was tall, so I didn't have to lower my head too much to kiss her eyelids, her cheeks. I loved her. I loved her for being strong enough to carry a knife and not being afraid to use it. We stood there, dancing to the house music and the cicada music, dancing like we hadn't at Alex's house.

I said, "I don't want you to leave."

She touched my hair. Her lips brushed my cheek, and she said, "That's what I do, Michael. I leave. It's the only thing I'm really good at."

"I don't want you to," I repeated.

"I haven't left yet," she said. "There's still time."

The bus pulled up to the stop. Her bus. She pulled away and started toward it, then turned back and held out her hand.

"Come with me tonight," she said. "Come home with me."

THIS YEAR

"Is Angela here?" I ask Karpe. I glance at my watch. Four o'clock. At the fairgrounds, they know I've left by now. "I mean, can I wait for her? I didn't want to go to the office in case . . ."

"In case you were on the news?" Karpe holds open the door. "You were. I mean, you will be. They had this promo: 'Runaway son spotted at fair, more at six.'"

"Maybe I should leave."

Karpe pushes the door open farther. "She'll be expecting you."

I step in. Their house is one of those Old Spanish houses in Coral Gables, where it feels like an army could invade and you'd still be safe. Karpe's alone, and I see books and papers scattered on the dining room table. The television hums in the background.

"Karpe, why are you so nice to me?" I remember blowing him off to go to the party that night last year. "I mean, I never did anything that nice for you."

"See, that's where you're wrong. It isn't every guy who'd fix you up with a contortionist."

I smile a little at that. "Tiffany still talks about you sometimes. She says you were the one who got her to quit smoking."

"The diseased-lung speech never fails. Maybe when

this is over, you'll take me back there."

I nod, but I know I'll never go back. I think Karpe knows too.

"Thing is, though," he says, "I probably didn't talk her into anything. Usually people know the right thing all along. They just need a little push sometimes."

"Maybe so." I have the feeling he isn't talking about Tiffany anymore.

"Listen," Karpe says. "I'm cramming for a trig midterm, but Angela should be here soon. You can talk to her then."

He takes me to the room with the TV. He shuts the door behind me, and I'm alone. I feel the bulge in my pocket, Cricket's money. I pull it out and smooth the bills. Fifty dollars—a ten, three fives, and twenty-five ones. I open my duffel bag to shove it in. The first thing I see is a slip of paper on top. I recognize Cricket's childish handwriting and a name: *Kirstie*.

The phone number has the 225 area code I've called so many times.

I stare at the paper, hearing her voice in my head saying *Happy birthday, Michael*. My birthday passed a week ago, with no one saying anything. I want to scream and jump and run downstairs to call her. But then I hear the clank of the jail door, the slam of Walker's body hitting the fireplace, and I know that Kirstie can't help me. Not now.

Still, I fold the paper and slide it into my wallet between Cricket's bills and my own.

LAST YEAR

When I was a kid, I wanted to live at the fair. I ran away from Mom once, planning to stay, planning to live on corn dogs and cotton candy and ride the rides forever. An hour later Mom picked me up at the Lost Children booth when my money ran out.

But people—lots of people—lived at the fair. There were maybe a hundred trailers in this walled-off section that was in the center of everything but hidden unless you looked.

It was after one o'clock when Kirstie and I got there, but lights blazed. A woman hung laundry outside a trailer, and a boy walked a shepherd mix, using a Baggie to pick up what it left. Heavy metal and country blared from competing radios, and no one seemed to mind. Kirstie said something to most people. But she held my hand.

When she reached one trailer, she thumped the door. "Home sweet home, and alone sweet alone!" She opened the door with a key from her money belt.

"So, rich boy, ever been in a trailer before?"

"Actually, my mom and I lived in one for a while, smartass. Then the city tore down the trailer park because it was bringing down their property values."

"Bet that made you feel good." Kirstie reached to turn on a light.

"I liked it there," I said. "It was comfortable."

The trailer was small and old, with saggy furniture that belonged on a garbage heap. I looked around like you do when you go to a new person's house, trying to find a part of the person who lives there. No sign of Kirstie's pre-carny life. A door to our left led into a bedroom, or, at least, a sort of closet with a bed in it. A few stuffed animals—the type that were small prizes in her game—were lined up on a faded yellow blanket. One wall of the main room was covered in postcards. A card from Mount Rushmore hung beside one of a giant stone chicken and another of musclemen on South Beach. Then I saw it—an old photo, barely visible underneath, of two little girls, one six, one maybe two. The older girl held a Chinese parasol. I looked away, feeling like I'd seen something she didn't want to show me.

I pointed at the SoBe postcard. "You've been here before?" I said.

"I've been everywhere. I've seen the world."

I stepped toward the wall and touched the photo, wondering if there was writing on the back.

"I just bought this trailer," she continued. "Got a good deal on it from a guy who used to tour with his tattooed-lady mother. Sold it to me when she died."

"Where'd you live before that?"

"Oh, you can rent a bed in a trailer with a bunch of other carnies for a few bucks a week. Some even sleep in their joints. But I needed someplace to be alone at night, where no one would mess with me."

Mess with me. I remembered my conversation with Cricket. I nodded, and she went on.

"So, I raised the money. I got a job in the off-season, waiting on drunks at a strip club. Not work I'm proud of, but the money was good."

I glanced at her. She was so pretty. "Just . . . waiting tables?"

She smiled. "They told me I could make big bucks dancing. But I've got stage fright, I guess . . . or something. Besides, you make good tips waitressing because guys think they have a chance with the waitresses—not that they did. I don't mind anyone looking at me. Look. Be happy. But I decide who touches me. I decide."

She turned and met my eyes. When she did it, her hair brushed my arm, and I felt a shower of sparks go up it. I was a little freaked out, being there with her. It didn't seem real.

But I said, "Can I touch you, Kirstie?"

She leaned toward me until we were so close it would have been impossible not to kiss her. She hadn't had beer at the party, and I was glad, because now she tasted sweet, like lipstick and lemonade, and then her hands were on me, running down my body, fumbling with the buttons of my 501s.

"I've never . . . ," I started, feeling like a little kid with her.

But she put her finger to my lips. "It's okay."

I picked her up like—I don't know—some cool guy in a movie and carried her through the door to her narrow bed. I dropped her onto it, sending the pile of stuffed Cliffords and Snoopys to the floor.

Outside I could hear the voices from other trailers. But I stopped listening or thinking. It felt fine, having something that wasn't about Mom, wasn't about Walker, but was just about me. Me and Kirstie. I kissed her again and was unbuttoning her last button when I heard a noise from the floor.

The beeper in my jeans pocket was going off.

It was two A.M.

THIS YEAR

It's two hours later when Angela comes in.

I say, "I left. I couldn't stay."

"I know. I heard about it on WIOD news."

"Do they know where I am?"

"No. But they're talking like they do."

"So what do I do?"

"You can stay with us."

"But what do I *do*?"

"That's up to you. I can take you in, let you stay awhile. But I can't do that without telling anyone about it. You're a minor, and it would be illegal. Or I can give you some money for a bus ticket out of town."

I feel Cricket's money, Kirstie's phone number in my pocket. I could go find her.

"But Michael, I don't recommend that. I've seen what happens to boys your age, out on their own."

I hear Walker's voice . . . *guys just waiting for a piece of your pretty, white ass.* I feel my eyebrows tighten. A year after his death, Walker still has the power to make me angry. I know I should tell Angela the truth. Even if she doesn't want me to tell anyone, I should tell her.

Angela's still talking, still going on about what would happen. "You've been lucky, this past year. But that luck won't last. The streets harden people. I'd hate to see that happen to you. I've really gotten to like you."

I smile, wondering if she'll still like me once she knows.

"Angela," I say, "I want them to know. I want to talk to them."

"You wouldn't necessarily have to. Your knowledge is limited. You left days before it happened. We could say—"

"Angela." I look down. "I was there the night it happened."

LAST YEAR

But the night one week before Walker died, I was at the emergency room at Mercy Hospital. I'd been there before.

An emergency room at night is like one of those old, silent movies where everyone moves really fast but no one seems to be going anywhere. A nurse pushed past me, and Kirstie gripped my elbow to pull me out of the way. I didn't see my mother yet. It was almost four.

It had taken a while to find a working phone at the fairgrounds. When I finally did, the answering machine picked up at home. I called five, six more times, hanging up, then redialing again and again to make sure, trying Mom's cell phone, too. My throat felt like someone had poured cement down there.

"Maybe you should just go home," Kirstie said.

"What if she's not home, though? Shit. I shouldn't have come here."

"This isn't your fault."

"What do you mean, it's not my fault? Who the hell else's fault is it?" I gripped the receiver and fumbled for more change.

Kirstie took the phone from me.

"Who are we calling to pick you up?" she said.

"Karpe." Without another thought. He was the one

person I knew who wouldn't bust my chops for calling him late.

Kirstie nodded and put coins in the slot. I gave her his number. She handed me the phone.

"'Lo?" Karpe's voice sounded strangled when he answered. Still, I explained where I was and why I needed to go home. He didn't say anything about the time. He didn't ask questions.

Until he got there.

"This has happened before?" he asked, like he knew the answer. Kirstie had waited with me at the entrance. I'd tried to tell her she didn't have to come, but she squeezed into Karpe's car. She held my hand.

I answered Karpe's question. "Yeah. It happens all the time."

He just nodded and sped over the rutted grass and muddy tire tracks of the fairground parking lot. When we reached Eighth Street, he said, "I hate this. Why do women put up with that shit? Why don't they just leave?"

Kirstie's grip on my elbow tightened. "They think they need a man, then worry what people will say if they leave."

"Shit," Karpe said.

The beeper in my pocket went off again.

• • •

When I called the number—Mom's cell phone—I got Walker.

"Where is she?" I demanded. My throat hurt with what I wanted to say, but I needed to make nice. I wanted him to talk to me.

"I just called to say you don't need to worry about her," he said. "She's fine."

"Where are you?"

"She had a little accident."

"Are you at the hospital? Let me talk to her."

"Nah, she's fine. You just stay with your little friends. I'll take care of things, like always."

Beep. The line went dead.

When I tried to call back, I got no answer.

"Change of plans," I told Karpe. "Head to the hospital."

We were already on the Rickenbacker Causeway, but Karpe found the next opening and made a U-ey.

"Let me guess," Kirstie said. "She fell down the stairs."

I nodded. "Or ran into a wall a few times. And he's with her, making sure she gets the story straight."

"Making sure she doesn't tell the truth, huh?" Karpe said. "That she ran into his fist."

When he saw the look on my face, he said, "Sorry."

• • •

The first person I saw when I walked into the E.R. waiting room was Walker. He was talking to a black nurse. He wore a button-down and looked like he'd showered and changed before coming. He laughed at something the nurse had said.

"I hear you," he said. "I'm the same way—overworked and underpaid. But I was just wondering if you could take a look. She's feeling bad. She fell a few hours ago. Seemed alright, then woke up hurting. I'm awfully worried about her, you know."

I looked and saw my mother. She was curled in a ball on an orange chair. She didn't have any injuries you could see. She usually didn't. No bruises or black eyes. But her skin was pale, and her lips looked like there was blood in them. I'd seen that before, more than once.

"What's wrong with her again?" the nurse asked Walker.

"She spit up some blood on the way here. Says her stomach hurts."

Next to me, Kirstie nudged Karpe. "Let's look for a candy machine. I'm starved."

She gave me a little look like *You going to be okay?* I nodded and walked over to where my mother was sitting.

"You're puking blood?" I touched her shoulder, and she drew away.

She glanced at Walker. "It's not that bad. I'm okay."

"Sure."

But she clutched her stomach, trying to hold the pain in. She looked at Walker, still talking to the nurse. He saw me, and his face sort of clouded up. But you wouldn't notice if you didn't know him. The nurse looked at my mother too.

"You're not okay," I said. "What the hell did he do this time?"

"Nothing."

"What the hell did he do this time?"

I wanted to shake her. She drew back and sat there, shivering. She didn't answer.

"Forget it," I said.

Because, in that one minute, I knew it. I knew that sooner or later he'd kill her. Maybe it would be a week or a month or ten years, but he would. And if I stuck around, I'd get to watch it, or maybe get killed too. Maybe I'd always known it. All the stuff I'd thought about wanting her to leave—it was just something I'd told myself. She'd never leave.

I swallowed. I didn't want to know that.

And it was that knowledge that made my fists clench, that made my throat tighten, that made me want to grab Walker by the collar and scream *You bastard!* and shake him.

I did none of it. Walker came over with the nurse.

"Look, honey. I told you I'd get someone over here."

Mom looked up. She met Walker's eyes, not the nurse's. They all ignored me.

The nurse started talking to Mom. "What's wrong, Mrs. . . . ?"

"Monroe," Walker filled in. "Lisa."

"Lisa." The nurse nodded. Her name tag identified her as Sherri Mastin. She moved away from Walker to the other side of my mother. "Talk to me, Lisa."

Mom glanced at Walker again. She wouldn't look at Sherri Mastin, and I remembered what she'd said, about wanting to be a nurse once. Finally she said, "My stomach. It hurts a little. It's not a big deal." She closed her eyes, and a tear seeped out of the side. She looked at Walker.

"It's okay." Walker came around and patted her shoulder. "You want me to tell her what happened?"

"It's better if I hear from the patient." Sherri Mastin got down on her haunches, making eye contact with my mother.

Mom shrank back. She looked at Walker. "I . . . I . . ."

"Can't you see she's in pain?" Walker demanded.

"I need to know what happened," Sherri Mastin said, while Mom snailed further and further into herself on the orange chair.

"I can tell you what happened."

It was my own voice. They all turned toward me. The nurse met my eyes, and I knew beyond doubt that she knew. Knew and was trying to get my mother to say it. Maybe she would tell the police, and they would finally do something about Walker. Well, I could tell her.

"He hit her. That's what he does—hits her in the stomach so no one can see, so there won't be any bruises."

"That's not true." Walker's voice was calm. "Michael, I know you're as upset about Mom as I am, but it's important for the doctors to know what really happened."

"That's why I'm telling them." I looked at Sherri Mastin. "He hit her. He hits her."

"Were you there when this happened, Michael?" Walker's voice was calm.

They were both looking at me again. Walker's eyes were understanding, *fake* understanding. And Sherri Mastin's eyes held that different understanding, that knowledge.

"Tell the truth, Michael," Walker said.

"Just tell us what happened," Sherri Mastin said. Her voice was so kind. I wanted to go to her, have her arms around me like a mother's. I started to say I'd been there. I'd seen Walker hit Mom. I was going to lie. It wasn't really a lie because I knew it was true.

"No." It was my mother. "No. My husband has never hit me." Her voice was stronger, like the lie gave her nourishment. "The bathroom floor was wet, and I slipped. I slipped."

There were tears in her eyes. I wondered if it was just the pain, or if it was the betrayal.

But before I could think too much about it, Walker had her in his arms, and Nurse Mastin was walking away, saying, "We'll run some tests. It will be at least an hour."

I ran after her.

"She's lying," I said. "He did it."

She turned to me. "Were you there?"

"No. I didn't need to be there this time. I was there a hundred other times."

"Why didn't she leave him then, that other hundred times?"

"I don't know."

"She won't leave him this time, either." She started to walk away again.

I ran after her. "What is wrong with you people?" I was screaming. "I'm telling the truth. How can you ignore it like that?"

I wanted to grab her, smash her to the floor, hold her ears, and *make* her listen to me.

She said, "Honey, how can I *not* ignore it? I have

over a hundred patients a night—traffic accidents, gun-shot victims, heart attacks, and maybe half a dozen domestic cases like your mother's." I started to say I didn't care about her other patients, but she held a hand up. "Sometimes the guy just dumps her at the door. That's the best because maybe, maybe she'll talk to me then. Or talk to a social worker if I can find one. Maybe she'll take a pamphlet for Safe Space and he won't beat the crap out of her when he finds it. But usu-ally it happens like that." She gestured at Walker. "He'll sit there, telling the story with that arrogant, smart-ass look on his face that says *I can make this dumb bitch do what I want* until I want to smack him. And she sits there like a dumb bitch, and I want to smack her, too."

"So you don't do anything?"

"I can't make them talk. But I try, like I tried with your mother. I try to get the story and put it on her chart. Try to get a record for the future in case—"

"In case he kills her?"

"I was going to say in case she leaves. But, yeah, there's those others, too."

"What others?"

"The ones it's too late for."

She glanced back at my mother and Walker. I looked too. He was still holding her, rocking her.

When I looked back at Sherri Mastin, she'd walked

away. I screamed after her.

"Don't you care?"

She stopped, looked at me, and with a gentleness in her voice that came from knowledge, she said, "I can't afford to care anymore."

She turned and walked away. I watched her back, down the hall. When she was gone, I turned toward Mom and Walker. Instead, I saw Kirstie waiting in the doorway with Karpe.

I ran to her.

THIS YEAR

"I know you were there, Michael."

Angela says it gently, like when I was eight years old and confessed to Mom that, yes, I was the one who'd uprooted the marigolds from in front of Old Lady Cagle's trailer—only to find out that Mom had already apologized and made arrangements for me to replant. I look at Angela, almost expecting her to pat me on the head and say she's proud of me for admitting it—like Mom did.

"Did Karpe tell you?"

"No. I just knew. You don't get very far in this business if you can't see the facts behind people's stories."

"So I guess this changes everything."

"It changes nothing. Yes, it's possible—probable— your mother's lawyers will want to speak with you about what happened that night. But you've committed no crime."

"But I was there. I . . ." I stop, unable to hear my words. Instead, I hear the screams, the sickening crunch of the fire poker breaking Walker's skull, the thud as his body hit the floor. My mind is red, red as my mother's bloody face and hands. But my own hands are clean.

Now I'm looking down at my shoes, rocking back and forth. Angela's beside me, her hand on my shoulder. "Listen," she says.

I say nothing, remembering the blood on my sneakers. I'd washed them before I left.

"Did you help her plan to kill him?"

I try to pull away from her. "No one planned anything. We—"

She keeps holding onto me. "Shh! Did you help her cover it up?"

"No. No. I just left."

"It's not a crime to watch someone die, Michael. Strange as it may seem, you can watch just about anything. There was a case in New York where a whole neighborhood saw a girl murdered, and nothing happened to them."

I stare at my shoes. But I think, *Didn't it? Didn't everything change forever for them?* Through the haze of blood and screams, I still see my mother's face and Walker's lifeless body.

"You've been running for a year now, Michael. Has it helped?"

I shake my head. "I want to tell them," I say. "I can't hide anymore. I want to do what I can for her."

When Angela doesn't say anything, I add, "I'm sure."

She nods. "I'll call Child Services. And then I'll call your mother's attorneys."

"I'm ready."

LAST YEAR

"I have to get out of here," I said.

Karpe looked across the waiting room. "But aren't we going to—"

"No. I need to go." I was already pulling Kirstie's arm. She didn't argue with me.

When we got to the parking lot, Karpe asked, "Am I taking you home or to school?"

"Neither."

"But there's school in"—Karpe checked his watch—"in two hours."

"You don't have to take me all the way to the fair. Just dump our asses at the Metrorail. We'll find the way."

"But I meant *you* have school in two hours."

"No, I don't. I'm not going there. I'm never going back there again." I walked faster toward the car, then turned to Karpe. "Look—thanks for picking me up. It was a pal thing to do, especially after the sucky way I acted yesterday. If you dump us at the train station, you should make school. I'm sorry . . . I'm sorry I made you lose sleep."

I was sorry about other stuff, too, but Karpe said, "Screw sleep. Michael, if you told someone, maybe—"

"I just did tell someone. It didn't help. Nothing will help."

"My dad's fiancée's a lawyer," Karpe said. "She could, maybe . . ."

But I shook my head.

"I'll take care of him," Kirstie told Karpe.

Karpe dropped us at the Vizcaya Metrorail station. It was nearly five, and the Wackenhut guard was hoisting the metal gate when we got there. I paid for both of us, and we climbed the stairs and waited for the first train.

"Do you want to talk about it?" Kirstie asked when we got on.

"No, I want to forget everything."

She wrapped her arms around me in reply.

* * *

Sometime in the early morning, there was a rainstorm. Thunder and wind shook the walls. I rolled over and looked around the dim room in confusion, seeing the outline of a yellow window, then the whole room coming into sharp focus with a lightning bolt. I felt a cool hand on my shoulder and remembered where I was, with Kirstie in her narrow, yellow-covered bed.

"It's okay," she said. "Sleep. It's only thunder."

"But . . ."

"You can stay with me as long as you like."

I rolled over and went back to sleep.

* * *

I woke Friday morning, alone in Kirstie's trailer, but knowing what I would do. I'd go with them. Everything I had in Miami was long gone already. Everything I had now was here. Monday morning, when the carnival packed up and left town, I would leave with it. Wherever they were going, I'd be going with them.

I looked at the old windup alarm clock on the TV table by Kirstie's bed. Almost noon. It took me a second to realize it was still Friday, still the day after the party and the hospital. The day before seemed so long ago. Even school. I felt a pang, realizing I'd never go to school again. But I had a new life with Kirstie now.

When I stepped out to look for her, a cold shower hit me. I wiped it from my eyes.

"Oops," Kirstie said, not apologetic at all. "Just cleaning up a little."

She held a hose and was hosing something off the side of the trailer. I ran down the steps and kissed her. I was soaking wet but she didn't pull away.

"Well, good morning to you, too," she said when we finally pulled apart.

"I'm staying," I said. "You were right."

"I so often am," she said, smiling. "You're sure? I wouldn't want to be contributing to the delinquency of a minor."

"I'm sure," I said. "I love you."

I stopped. I'd been avoiding the words for a week. Now they were stuffed into the space between us, like an exploded airbag. Separating us. I held my breath. Please don't think I'm a stupid kid. Please let this moment go by. She didn't have to say it back. I'd have settled for her not laughing.

But part of me needed her to love me too.

"You don't have to say that," she said. "It's not required."

"I know it's not, but I love you. You've changed my life. You've saved me."

"You saved yourself." She turned away. When she looked back, she said, "We'll talk to Corbett about a job for you."

• • •

It was amazing how quickly it happened. In the next two days I talked to Corbett about an under-the-table job, and Kirstie set me up with a fake ID that said I was eighteen and gave my name as Robert Frost. I started on a mustache.

I slept in Kirstie's bed. I didn't ask her to tell me she loved me. She didn't tell me, either.

The other carnies acted differently since I was staying. Some, who'd treated me like a harmless tagalong, now looked at me suspiciously. Others, who'd treated me with suspicion, were friendly now that I was staying.

I didn't go home for two days. But I knew I had to go back, to say good-bye. I planned to do it Sunday, the day the fair closed.

I woke early that morning and put on a borrowed souvenir T-shirt. I'd get my clothes from home too. I tried not to wake Kirstie, getting up. We'd been up until after three, and the fair opened early that day. I stood, watching her in the dim light. Eighteen days I'd known her. Eighteen days ago I'd been a mess, trapped with Mom and Walker, unable to move, unable to leave, worrying every day I'd snap, feeling like I had nothing to lose by doing it.

Now it was all changed. I had Kirstie. I had friends, too, a job, a life ahead of me instead of just behind. And more than that, I'd made a decision. I wasn't trapped anymore. I was a man in every sense of the word.

But was I? I felt guilty about leaving. Yet I knew there was nothing I could do by staying. Maybe my staying even made it worse. So many of the fights Mom and Walker had were about me in some way. Because of me. It would be better if I left. I was kidding myself if I thought I could help by staying.

I opened the trailer door and stepped outside. The air was cool and clean smelling. The light hit Kirstie's face, and she sort of cringed against it. I started to close the door behind me.

"Where are you going?"

"I'm going home. I mean, I'm going to my mother's house."

"Don't leave." Her still-sleepy voice was like a little kid's.

"I'm not leaving. I'm just going to pack my things, to say good-bye."

She was sitting up now. "Don't. Please don't. If you go, they'll suck you back in. They'll make you stay, and. . . ." She fumbled with the sheet now, pulling it around her.

"I have to. I'm not staying, but I have to say good-bye. Don't you wish you'd said good-bye to anyone?"

She looked away. Finally, she said, "I said good-bye to Erica that day when I left her at the funnel cakes. She didn't know it was for forever, but I did."

"But . . ."

"If I'd said good-bye for real, I couldn't have left. I could have left Dad, that's for sure. But not Erica."

"Well, I am leaving." Though, even as I said it, I felt my resolve slipping. "I don't know what will happen to my mother, but sorry, I need to tell her I'm going so she won't put out an APB. And I need my stuff."

"Cricket can loan you clothes. Life's all about leaving things behind anyway. What's a few T-shirts?"

"Cricket's, like, five-four." I let the door close and walked close to her. "I need to do this, Kirstie. But I'll be back." I sat on the bed and put my arms around her. She felt motionless as an ice block. "I'll be back."

"I love you too, Michael."

I looked at her, and for the first time, she wasn't the girl I knew, strong, confident, able to take on anyone even if she had to use a knife to do it. She looked scared, waiting for my answer.

"I'm coming back, Kirstie. I promise."

Then I walked to the door and opened and closed it again before I could change my mind.

THIS YEAR

I find Karpe in his room, the trig test forgotten, watching television.

"They know nothing, *nada*." He points to the screen even though the news isn't on anymore. It's nine thirty, and he's watching some show on the WB.

"I told Angela," I tell him. "I told her I was there the night it happened."

"They tried to talk to some carnies, but none of them would comment. They didn't want to be on television." He hears what I said and adds, "Do you feel better, telling?"

"Not a whole lot. I don't think I'll ever feel better."

"You sure are hard on yourself."

"Shouldn't I be? I mean, I lived there two years, watching it happen, watching him beat her up. And now, I'm still watching. Do you have any idea how shitty that feels?"

Karpe reaches for the remote and snaps off the television.

"Yes," he says.

"Right."

"No, really. I know. When my parents first got divorced, I lived with my mom awhile. And she had a boyfriend who . . . had problems." He looks away. "That's why I moved in with Dad. I was in all kinds of therapy at the time, and the main thing they were telling me was it wasn't my fault. But I never totally believed it, you know?"

I nod. It reminded me of what Kirstie had said. "When did it happen?"

"When I was eleven. Sixth grade. That's when they got together."

I realize what he's saying. "The year we stopped being friends."

"Right. I pretty much disconnected from everyone that year. I never blamed you or anyone. You couldn't have known."

"But you knew about my mom," I say, remembering how Karpe befriended me when everyone else was ditching in droves. Karpe had known, too, for the best reason. He'd experienced it himself. I'd been so sure no one could understand.

"I suspected," he says. "I knew the signs. But I didn't really know until that night at the hospital. That night with . . . what was her name?"

"Kirstie."

"Kirstie. That night when you left with her."

"I wish I'd never gone back to the house."

"Why did you?"

"I barely even remember anymore."

But I do remember. I remember so strongly that I feel like I could go back, change direction, if only I thought about it hard enough.

LAST YEAR

It took me the whole morning to get to Key Biscayne. I wondered if Kirstie was right, if I should just disappear without a word. I had enough money now to buy a carny's wardrobe, and I was staying with Kirstie anyway. But finally I decided that no, I had to say good-bye.

I got home midday, when I'd be least likely to see Walker. He'd be at work or, if not, out on his sailboat. I didn't make a sound going to my room to pack. I knew how to be quiet. The surf would have drowned me out anyway. I packed a duffel with only what I needed, some clothes and sneakers, a few photos. I added a slightly deflated football to the top, then took it out. I'd have no room for extras now.

When I finished packing, I went to Mom's room.

As usual, she was stitching.

She rushed to me. "I was so worried, Michael. Walker said your bed wasn't slept in Thursday. Then yesterday and the day before." When I didn't answer, she said, "But you're back."

The ocean was so loud. "I'm leaving again."

"Walker will be home soon for dinner. Maybe tomorrow would be a better day to go out."

"I mean I'm leaving." I looked behind me at the

green duffel I'd left in the doorway. She saw it too. "I'm leaving for good."

The fabric she was embroidering fell from her hands.

"Oh, no, Michael. No."

"I'm sorry."

"But what will I do?" She came closer. I noticed her walk, that she favored one leg.

"Same as you do with me here. Nothing. You wouldn't let me help." I thought of Nurse Mastin saying, *I can't afford to care anymore.*

"But I've done this all for you."

"Don't lay that on me!" I screamed. "I can't believe you'd say that."

"How can you leave me with . . . I mean, Michael, it's been bad. At the office. His partners cut him out. It happened Thursday. The day he . . ."

I remembered that time at Walker's office, those two guys on the elevator. They'd been talking about Walker. *The old man*, they'd called him. But I didn't feel sorry for him. He was responsible for what he did, same as I was responsible for what I did.

I started to say there'd always be something to blame for Walker's rages, but I stopped. I was here to say good-bye.

Still, I had to try one last time.

"Come with me," I said.

She shook her head like I knew she would. "I can't. You know I can't."

"You won't."

"It would be kicking him when he's down, leaving now."

"He's the one who kicks, not you." Then I stopped talking. It was no use. The wind was whistling across the beach. I stared at my mother. The balcony door slammed shut.

We both looked out, silent.

"I'm going now." I picked up the duffel and gave her a kiss on the cheek. "I'm sorry."

I started to leave the room. I couldn't do anything for her, I reminded myself. *But you could be here*. My eyes stung with the cold salt air that hung in the room.

I didn't look back.

"I'm pregnant," she said.

I turned, sending my duffel into the wall.

"What?"

"I haven't told him yet. I was going to Thursday, but then . . . I don't know what will happen when he finds out."

I still didn't look at her. I looked out the closed balcony door. I felt cold and sick.

"So you can't leave," she said. Did her voice hold a

note of triumph? "You wouldn't leave us—your little brother or sister—alone here, would you?"

"How long have you known?"

"I wasn't sure until Thursday. I did my grocery shopping, and bought a test. But I thought so before then. I've known for weeks, really."

I thought of her, clutching her stomach Thursday night at Mercy. Outside, the dark waves churned.

"I need you, Michael. I know you're a good kid, a responsible kid."

What about your responsibility to me? But it was no use, no use trying to get her to go with me either. There was nothing left but a decision. Stay. Or go.

Below, I heard the garage door open.

"There's Walker, Michael. I have to start dinner."

She looked at me, a question in her eyes.

I carried the duffel bag back to my bedroom.

THIS YEAR

"I should have left that night," I tell Karpe now. "If I had, none of this would have happened."

"You thought you could protect her."

"Some protection. If I left, maybe she wouldn't be in jail."

"Maybe she'd be dead."

I think about that a minute. It makes me feel better, but it doesn't make me feel good.

"I never heard about a baby," Karpe says after a moment. "I mean, on the news or anything. Did she—"

"No," I say. "No, you wouldn't have heard about it."

He waits for me to continue, but I don't. Finally, he says, "So, what happened?"

"The next morning, when I was supposed to be in school, I went back to talk to Kirstie. To tell her good-bye instead."

LAST YEAR

The fair was over, leaving. Parts of rides lay on the ground like dinosaur skeletons. I knew if I came back the next day, there'd be nothing but candy wrappers and melted ice cream, and the whole thing would be like the memory of a dream.

Cricket waved to me from what was left of the double Ferris wheel. "You made it. Kirstie was worried about you."

"Where is she?"

"Around. Probably where the midway was."

I walked toward the midway. All the game booths were closed, shuttered, some hooked to trucks that would pull them to the next town. The place looked barren without all the people. I didn't see Kirstie anywhere. I reached her joint. It was shuttered, the wheels on.

I started to walk away, then caught a gleam of gold underneath the trailer. I walked closer and stooped to look.

I picked up a string of golden beads. The theme of that year's fair was Mardi Gras. The beads were a give-away. I held them up, feeling their weight. Then I pressed them to my lips before reaching for my pocket.

"You're not coming with us, are you?"

I looked up. It was Kirstie.

"No, I . . ." It wasn't how I'd wanted to tell her. "You have to understand. It's not that I don't want to go with you. I do, but—"

"She needs you," she said dully.

"Yeah." I walked closer, loving her and unable to believe I'd never see her again.

"I understand." The wind blew. She wrapped her arms around herself. It was morning, cool, and she was wearing only a T-shirt and jeans. Standing against the shuttered game joint, she looked like a pioneer woman standing by her covered wagon, ready to go wherever life would take her. I wanted to go too, but I couldn't. "Your family needs you. I don't."

"It's not that."

"It's exactly that," she said. "I understand. I even envy you. I remember what it was like, having people need me."

"I need you. I just can't give in to that right now. I know there's nothing I can do, but she's my mother. My family. And I can't . . . not know what happens to her, even if it's bad. I can't deal with not knowing. I'm not strong like you are. I'm sorry."

"Never apologize. Remember that."

I moved close to her. "I'm sorry for *me*."

"You'll be fine too."

The clanking continued in the background. This should have been the day I began working, the first day I learned to dismantle the Tilt-a-Whirl. And tomorrow I should have been on my way to a new town, someplace I'd never seen before.

I could still go, I realized. I was free to go, same as before. I could tell Kirstie I changed my mind and just go with her.

Instead, I kissed her one last time.

"See you next year?" I said. "Same place?"

"Maybe so." She didn't look at me. Another gust of wind, and she held herself harder. I took off my gray Key Biscayne High Dolphins sweatshirt and handed it to her.

"Stay warm," I said.

She hesitated a second, then took it, holding it, pressing the fleece to her face, her nose, before finally putting it on. "Thank you." She looked at the stand beside her, where they were packing up a giant ice cream cone. "I really have to go help now."

I nodded, and she walked away.

• • •

That was the last time I saw Kirstie. When I met up with the carnival a week later, she was gone.

THIS YEAR

"Parker House." The voice that answers the phone is abrupt and has a southern accent. Angela's making phone calls, and Karpe's vegging in front of the WB's Tuesday night lineup. But I'm thinking of Kirstie. I'm planning on doing something big. I can't do it without talking to Kirstie first.

"Can I speak to Kirstie Anderson?"

"Who's calling?"

"Friend of hers. I . . . what kind of place is Parker House, anyway?"

"Drug rehab. I need your name."

Drug rehab? I remember the story she told me about her past. "Michael. Tell her it's Michael Daye. Is she . . . ?"

"Michael?"

The voice softens, and I recognize it.

"Kirst?" My face and throat turn inside each other until I can barely talk. "Kirstie?"

"Didn't think I'd ever hear your voice again."

"I've been looking for you since—"

"You were right, Michael. You can't run, not really. I couldn't anymore either. I just didn't have the heart for it, you know?"

I hold the phone harder.

248

"After you left, I left too. I went home to find Erica. My sister."

"Did you find her?"

"Yeah, right here in Lennox. She was having some problems, same type I had at that age. But now it's getting better. We're here. Michael, I'm so glad I went home. I don't know what would have happened to her if I hadn't. My father . . . well, he wasn't helping her any."

"And you're . . . ?"

"I'm fine. Great, really. Got a job here, answering phones and keeping track of stuff. I got my GED. I'm thinking of maybe junior college in a year or so. And they let me live here, to be with her. I promised I'd never leave again. That was our deal."

Junior college. It sounds so normal. Not like the Kirstie I knew, Kirstie in a green T-shirt with carnival lights in her hair.

"I missed you," I say, my mind still not totally wrapping around the idea that the voice on the other end of the phone is hers, is all the way in Louisiana. I feel like I could go back to the fairgrounds right now and find her. "Every day, I missed you."

"I know. But it was the right thing to do. You taught me that."

"Taught you what?" I say, surprised.

249

"After you left, I started thinking about what you said about family. I thought family was just something you grew through and got over. But it's not. I wanted to live without responsibility, but when you do that, you live without having anyone to care about you, too. It's like you're not a real person anymore, and I wanted to be real. Now I know I'm not responsible for everything that happens. I wasn't responsible for what happened to my mother or how my dad was—just what I did. That's all, but that's enough."

"I loved you, Kirstie. I still . . . I mean, it's been a year and I never forgot, you know?"

"Yeah." Her voice becomes a whisper. "Yeah, me too. But I need to go now. Someone's here."

"Can I call again?"

"Yes, I'd like that. Or come see me. I have to go."

She hangs up. In the other room Angela's still on her cell phone, and every inch of me aches to bail, to go outside, to get on a bus and head for Louisiana. Instead, I go back to Karpe's room.

●　●　●

"Julian?" Angela's voice comes over the house intercom system. "Is Michael up there?"

"Yeah, I'm here," I say.

"I spoke to them." She hesitates. "We need to talk."

"I'll be right down."

I start toward the door, then turn back. "Angela knows, right? About what you told me?"

"Yeah, my dad told her. I think he thought I'd be freaked out when he got married."

"Did the guy . . . I mean, did he do anything to you?"

Karpe shakes his head. "Same as your guy. Just the stuff he did to my mom. That, and the stuff I did to myself." He reaches for the remote. "You better go down now."

I nod and leave. I'm halfway down the stairs when I hear the television: *Possible plea bargain in murder case.*

I break into a run.

LAST YEAR

I didn't go to school Tuesday after I left the carnival. Wednesday either. I knew I'd have to go back sometime. Skipping more would only make things worse. But I couldn't get out of bed. I woke alone, mornings, and thought of Kirstie, waking alone someplace else, someplace I'd never even seen.

Then I'd roll over and go back to sleep.

I was a shadow around the house those days too. I didn't come down to meals with Mom and Walker. I didn't talk to Mom, who'd given up even on embroidery and spent her days staring out at the ocean. Me, I mostly locked myself in my room, listening to CDs, and went to bed at seven every night.

Wednesday she came into my room. She gave a little sniff at the door (I'd given up showering, too), then sat on the edge of my bed.

"You need to go to school, Michael."

"Why?"

"It's the law, for one thing. And Walker will get mad."

"It's always about that, isn't it?"

"And I want you to have a future."

Well, I don't. But instead, I said, "Did you tell him yet?"

"Tell him what?" But then, she smiled. "I did. He was really happy."

"Really?" It wasn't like Walker to be happy, especially if things were going badly at work.

"He says it will be like a new start—this baby, his new firm. He's starting a new practice with lower overhead."

"I don't care about his practice or his overhead."

She ignored me. "He wants us all to be a family. If you could just *try*. Go to school."

I wanted her off my bed. "How's your stomach? Still hurt where he hit you?"

"Michael . . ."

"I'll go tomorrow. Get off my bed."

"Have dinner with us."

I glanced at my watch. Six forty-five. That's what this was about—putting on a show for Walker at dinner. But I knew I should, knew I'd have to eventually.

"I'll do that tomorrow too. I promise. I don't feel good today."

She nodded and stood. "Okay. Tomorrow."

She left, going downstairs to finish preparing dinner. I stripped to my boxers, turned out the light, and lay in bed, listening to the ocean. It was so rough, I could hear it through the closed window. I thought of Kirstie again, wherever she was.

I went to sleep that night knowing what Kirstie had meant when she'd talked about having nothing left to lose. Everything I'd wanted for sixteen years was gone—football, my friends. My whole future. And now the life I'd wanted to trade it for was gone too. I thought there was nothing left to lose.

I was wrong. Big-time wrong.

THIS YEAR

"Plea bargain?" I say to Angela when I walk into her study.

She nods. "Fifteen years."

Fifteen years. In jail. My stomach feels like that day Walker punched me. I can't breathe.

Angela's still talking. "It took me a while to get in touch with her lawyer."

"Shit. She did it for me, because I was there . . . to keep me from saying anything, to keep me from—"

"You can't know that, Michael."

"I do know it. She was trying to protect me." I think of the years she wouldn't let me play ball. And I hear Kirstie's voice on the phone, Kirstie's voice saying, *You can't run. Not really.*

I look at Angela. She's obviously thinking my mother didn't protect me enough. But she doesn't know it all.

She says, "I know it's hard. But it's not a bad deal, Michael. She won't serve the whole fifteen years, probably."

"But what about battered-spouse syndrome? What about her defense? Shit, she doesn't belong in jail. She didn't do anything wrong."

"She killed him, Michael. Fifteen years isn't that bad.

And this way, you don't have to testify, don't have to subject yourself to—"

You can't run. . . .

"You don't understand, Angela. She didn't kill him. I did."

LAST YEAR

That night, I dreamed I was dismantling rides at the fair. I was using a hydraulic drill. Beside me, someone was hammering. Every once in a while I heard the pounding, even over the shriek of my drill. But mostly it was the screaming, the screaming, filling my head until it was about to explode in a wall of flame.

I woke, sweating, shaking, not knowing where I was. Everything was blackness, and the hammering, the shrieking, just kept going on and on.

The screams came from below me, downstairs. It wasn't like before. It was much more, filling the air, like death. Then I was jumping from bed, stumbling toward the stairs, slipping on cold marble. I don't even remember running down, just landing.

Downstairs, lights blazed yellow. The runner on the hallway table was ripped. Objects that had been on top of it lay broken, on the floor.

I didn't stop. The cold heat moved me.

Another scream. Then it all stopped.

I was in the doorway of Walker's study. I heard my breath rasping in my ears. Walker was yelling, but I couldn't make out the words. Only my own breath, louder now.

And I saw them. He had her up against the fireplace,

257

punching her in the stomach like he did. With each blow, her head slammed the coral fireplace. He was going to kill her. He'd kill her. God, it was never going to end unless I ended it or Walker did.

Then my eyes went to her stomach.

What was he doing to the baby?

I don't remember lurching forward. But I must have, grabbing the iron fireplace poker—so cold—aiming it at Walker's skull, bringing it down, again. Again. I don't remember her screams. I didn't hear them.

But I remember the feeling, the shock to my arm as it hit hard bone, over and over. Then the relief as the bone crushed in. As Walker's skull broke and let me inside. The warmth of the spattering blood hitting me. I was on the floor. This was the only way it would end, the only way was if I ended it.

He was on the floor. I kept hitting him. Then he was just there, motionless.

Dead?

I stopped and stared at the nightmare face that had been Walker. I held the fire poker up, ready to hit him again if he moved. But he didn't.

I was glad he was dead. I was glad. Glad.

Glad.

I dropped the fire poker, and it clattered to the floor.

THIS YEAR

"I killed him," I tell Angela. In my arm I can still feel the vibrations, the cramp in my hand where I held the poker, the airy exhilaration of seeing him fall. Then the horrible realization. I was a killer.

At her desk Angela is completely still, quiet.

Behind me I hear a voice.

"You were protecting her," Karpe says. "Her and the baby."

"The baby," I say, dully. "Yeah. The baby."

LAST YEAR

So much blood. A puddle below Walker's head and small droplets all over, some as high as the ceiling. And other stuff. Images flipping past my eyes like the shadows on a movie screen. My mother crouched over Walker. The fire poker in my hand. Walker's body, still now. My mother shook him. She wasn't crying. He didn't move, didn't speak.

"Oh, my God, Michael. Oh, God, what have you done?"

I couldn't speak. Her face was covered with blood. I didn't feel it on my own face, but it must have been there. I couldn't be clean.

"I had to," I said, feeling strong. "He'd have killed you. Don't you understand? He'd have killed you, or killed the baby."

She'd sunk forward onto Walker's bloody body, embracing, cradling him. She moaned.

She stayed there a long time. Finally she said, "There's no baby, Michael."

"What?"

"There was never a baby. There was never one. Never. I only told you that so . . ."

"So I wouldn't go," I finished for her.

"I didn't think . . . oh, God." It was a sob. She looked

down at Walker's bloody face and recoiled. Then she was frantic, removing her shirt so she was only in her skirt and bra. She started trying to wrap the shirt around Walker's head. She couldn't do it, and his head flopped onto the floor.

"What do we do?" I still hadn't moved. My heart was ramming against my ribs, and I felt like it might stop beating entirely. I stared; the horror of what I'd done hit me like a sudden wave. "I killed him. Oh, God, I killed him." His head was bloody, unrecognizable. A smell filled the air. Blood. I even tasted it in my mouth, and I wondered if I'd swallowed it somehow, and suddenly it was like I realized what it was, like it had come into focus, Walker's head, Walker's bloody face, and Mom trying to cover it. I felt the sickness well up in my throat. I crouched and puked on the tile. I tried not to look at him again. I was choking on the blood-filled air, and I couldn't move. I couldn't move. Then I did. I put my hands to my face, and they were clean.

"I don't know. I don't know. . . ." She tried to wrap the shirt again. She was crying, gritting her teeth. She was covered in his blood.

Then her face changed, somehow, and she said, "You have to go."

"What?"

"I did this." She let go of Walker and stood, trembling.

She was all covered with his blood. "I did it, and that's what I'll tell them."

"But . . ."

"You have to go. You have to let me do this for you. You're my baby."

And suddenly I felt tired. Tired enough to lie down on the floor beside Walker and never get up again. Too tired to resist.

"No, I can't let you." I started toward her.

"Don't move!" Her voice was sharp. I looked at the Oriental rug, where my bloody footprints were about to be. "Wait there."

I stood, staring at my clean hands, while she went, so carefully, and found a towel for me to walk across, another for over Walker's face. I threw it onto him, feeling the puke welling up again but keeping it down.

"I need to do this, Michael. You need to let me. I'll explain that he was killing me, that he beat me. It will be okay. I won't go to jail. It happens all the time."

And it was decided. I went upstairs, showered, and put the towel, bath towel, my underwear, which had only a few drops of blood on it, and my other laundry into the washing machine. I waited until the water ran hot over my hands, then added twice the normal amount of detergent. I found my still-packed duffel and brought it to the front door.

My mother had put her energy into cleaning. When I reached the study, the puke was gone, but there was still blood. So much blood. And the smell. I could see the outline of footprints, her footprints, all over. I started toward the body.

"Michael, no!"

I spun.

"Don't touch anything." Her hair, her face were still covered with blood.

"We could bury him," I said. "Or throw him in the ocean. We could leave town and not tell anyone. He doesn't work at the firm anymore. No one will be waiting for him." I couldn't believe it yet. Everything had changed so horribly. It seemed like there had to be some way to fix it, to go back in time.

"There's no way to cover this. They'll know he's dead. They'll know he's dead, and they'll know I killed him."

"But . . ."

"*I* killed him. You have your life ahead of you. I have nothing. Nothing. It's all over anyway. I've ruined everything."

I recognized the mother of my childhood, the woman who hadn't wanted me to play ball, hadn't wanted me to get hurt. Where had she been all this time?

I waited for the wash cycle to finish and about half the dry, then packed the steamy, damp clothes into my duffel and started toward the only place I could think of. Julian Karpe's. I went on foot after I told Mom to wait half an hour to call the police.

I was halfway to Karpe's before it hit me again: I'd killed a man.

THIS YEAR

"Where did you go that night?" Angela asks, and I can see from her face that she's accepted it, maybe always knew.

"I came here, Angela."

She fixes her eyes on Julian. "So you . . . knew all this?"

I say, "I lied and told him my mother did it, like she said. I had to tell him that much, to explain why he couldn't tell anyone."

"I knew," he confirms. "At least, I thought you probably did it."

I stare at him. "But you helped me anyway?"

"I know what it's like to feel trapped, to feel like there's no way out."

"I walked here," I say to Angela, "then he drove me two hours to West Palm Beach to catch a Greyhound."

Angela looks at Karpe, assessing. "And you went back to school and told everyone you hadn't seen him since that Thursday?"

"He was a good friend," I say.

"Or an accessory after the fact, depending on how you look at it."

"I won't get him in trouble," I say.

"No," Angela says. "No, I know you won't."

"You knew I did it," I say to her. "Didn't you?"

"I suspected."

"Why?"

"It didn't seem likely to me that your mother would have beaten someone to death with a blunt object. Knowing my own mother, I just couldn't picture it. And . . ."

"And . . ?"

"You came back. I didn't think you'd come back unless you had something to say."

I nod. It's true, I realize. I have known all along I'd tell. The whole time I've been talking, I've been standing, leaning against the chair across from Angela's desk. But now, my legs feel tired, so tired, like they won't support me. And then, everything begins to go black.

• • •

When I come to, I'm on the floor. Angela and Karpe kneel over me.

"Are you okay?" Angela says.

"No," I say. "I mean yes. I mean . . . I have to tell them."

Angela touches my shoulder. "Your mother clearly doesn't want you to. That hasn't changed."

"No," I say. "I have to tell."

She nods. "Then let's do it."

THE NEXT DAY

Justifiable homicide. That's what the state attorney tells the judge after hearing my confession, talking to my mother in jail, my mother's lawyers, Angela, and me.

"It explains the blood spatter," one of the lawyers for the state, a guy named Miller, said to another, after I told them what happened. The other two attorneys glared at him, but he said, "Well, we've all been talking about it."

"The what?" I asked Angela.

"The blood-spatter evidence," Angela explained. "The experts try to figure out what happened by the way the blood spurted from the wounds. Your mother says she was fighting Walker off when it happened, and they're trying to show that she snuck up behind him and killed him. But the way the blood spattered didn't mesh with either story. She was covered in blood when the police arrived, and she shouldn't have been if she did it—just like you weren't. The state has ignored that evidence."

"Blood spatter is a very inexact science," the young assistant state attorney said defensively. "And we accepted her confession."

"Even though you didn't believe her about anything else?"

"Obviously we didn't have all the facts before us." He looked at me.

"So you thought he was going to kill her?" one of the older state attorneys, a woman who introduced herself as Toussaint, said.

I nod. "He had her against the fireplace. He was beating her head against the stone."

"But he'd done that all before, according to what you said."

"This time was different." I remembered the screams, the ripped runner. "I'd been there a dozen times when he did this, but this time was different. I really thought he'd kill her. I wouldn't . . . I mean, I never wanted to kill anyone. But I thought he was going to kill her."

And something about my face must have persuaded her. She said, "And you would be willing to give a sworn statement to that effect?"

"Yes."

For the first time in a year, I felt like I could breathe.

• • •

And so the next day I'm sitting in court. I watch Toussaint's lips as she says, "In light of new evidence, which we've just received, the State will *nolle pros* this matter."

Toussaint glances over at the reporters when she says this. There are gasps, and I see the reporter with the sketch pad switch his attention from my mother to Toussaint.

Me, I'm sitting in the back of the courtroom with Angela. We walked in with the state attorneys and the security guards. I still have the beard, but I borrowed some khakis and a blue jacket and tie from Karpe so I don't look like a carny anymore, though I don't look like Michael Daye anymore either, which is about right. The jail people brought my mother in separately, so I haven't spoken to her. I don't know whether she's seen me yet.

I watch her from behind. With her brown hair and her navy blue suit, she doesn't seem like what the reporters have been calling her. She sits quietly, her hands clasped before her face. I wish I could see her eyes, but she looks only at Toussaint.

"Newly acquired evidence?" the judge asks when the noise dies down. "Mind telling me what that is?"

Toussaint says, "We're still sifting through it ourselves, Your Honor."

"Can you tell me whether anyone else will be charged in this case?" The judge looks directly at me when he says that.

"No, Your Honor. We believe the new evidence will show that this is a case of justifiable homicide."

My mother's lawyer hugs her, but now my mother's eyes look for me.

THREE HOURS LATER

I still haven't seen her. Angela and I sit in Angela's car outside the jail, waiting for my mother to fill out the paperwork, which will release her forever. The top is up to escape the curious glances. But the windows are open. I feel the sun and breeze on my face.

"Happy?" Angela says.

I stare at the sun glinting off the barbed wire. "Happy isn't exactly the right word. I mean, I'm relieved, but . . ."

"But what, Michael? Because I was thinking we did pretty good in there."

"You did . . . but it's hard to explain. Sometimes I feel like I'll never be happy again."

She frowns. "You're free to be happy, Michael, free to go on with your life, play football, go to college. It's over now."

I picture myself, walking into school and explaining that I want to be on next year's football team. Then I think of the cheers the other side would make up about me.

"I guess," I tell Angela. "But it's different. *I'm* different. Most people, they go their whole lives thinking, *I could never do that. I could never kill another human being*, knowing they could never use their hands on someone and make the life go away. I used to know that about myself."

Angela nods, understanding. "You thought you knew."

"Right. But now I know I could do it. I *have* done it." In my arm I can feel the motion of it, the tightness of my arm as I hit bone. "Sometimes, I can even feel the pressure of his skull before it cracked. And when I get mad at someone now and say, 'I could kill him,' I think maybe I'm not just exaggerating. Maybe I could. I wish I didn't know all that about myself. I wish I could just feel like whether I make first team next year is important. And . . ."

I stop. I don't know what else I wish, actually. That everything could go back to the way it was before, and we'd be trapped with Walker? That I'd run away with the fair when I said I would, and then maybe it would be my mother who died, and Walker who was charged with her murder? No.

I say, "The fair leaves town tomorrow."

"Will you be with it?" Angela asks. "I guess they'd take you back now."

"I don't know if they would," I say, thinking of the system of secrets and lies at the fair. Now that they all know, it changes everything. "But no, I'm not going back. I can't keep running away. Wherever I go, this will always be part of me. Nothing will ever be the same."

She puts a hand on my shoulder. "Listen to me. You lived with that bastard for—what?—two years?"

She means Walker. I nod.

"And now he's dead, but he's still beating you up."

"It wasn't me he beat up. It was—"

"Maybe he didn't beat you up in a physical sense. But he beat you up. That's what these guys do—they beat people up on the inside, where no one can see the bruises. I look at you and I see a kid who's beat up, and who's still being beat up."

"I can't do anything about that."

"You can. You can let the bastard die. Whether you make first string *is* important, because that's the future. That means you've moved on. And that's what you need to do—move on. The state isn't charging you with murder. They've ruled it a justifiable homicide. That means a killing that is justified. You took a life to save a life, Michael. They didn't need to put you in jail for that."

I shake my head. "I'm in jail now. In my head, where it matters." I glance at her hand on my shoulder. "But thank you for doing this for me."

"I did it for a reason, Michael—because I knew you did it, but I also knew you were innocent. I hope someday, you'll realize it too."

Then she nods toward the jailhouse door, and I see my mother coming out. I open the door and run toward her.

EPILOGUE:
SUMMER BEFORE SENIOR YEAR

Last night I dreamed I was playing football. In my dream I finally made first string. It's the last game of the season. The score's tied. We're lined up at the ten. The center snaps the ball. I fade back, looking for my receiver. Tristan. I pass it to him, and I'm watching the ball soar toward the end zone, when suddenly something in the stands catches my eye, a bit of green mixed in with all the crimson and gray.

It's Kirstie. The green is the same green T-shirt she wore the first time I saw her. She stands in the middle of the screaming, cheering crowd, calm and alone. But when she sees me, she waves.

Her eyes meet mine, then travel downward. I follow them in time to see Tristan catch the pass, scoring the winning TD. When I look back into the stands, Kirstie is gone.

I awake to Kenny and Footy, screaming on Y-100's morning show. I'd set the alarm for early this morning, five thirty A.M. Today Coach will post the rosters for this year's teams. If all goes as planned, part of last night's dream will be reality. I should finally make starting QB this year.

But I won't be throwing any passes to Tristan. All my

friends graduated back in June. They've gone away to college, mostly. Julian Karpe, who's staying in town to attend U of M's six-year medical program, says he'll see me around. But probably he'll move on with his life like everyone else.

Me, I'll be a year behind them. I finished my sophomore year in summer school, then started last fall as a junior. The year off doesn't affect my eligibility for high school or college football, and—as Coach says—that's the important thing.

But there are other things. It was weird going back to school at first, with everyone knowing what happened. Some people avoided me. Others went out of their way to be nice. A couple of girls I'd never met slipped love letters through the slats of my locker, but I got some hate mail, too. I pretty much deal with it, because that's all you *can* do really. After a while, it died down. Sometimes I'll be at the mall or on the beach and I'll see someone looking at me but, you know, trying *not* to look at me. It happens less often than it used to, though.

I take the world's fastest shower and head downstairs for breakfast. My mother's already in the kitchen when I get down.

We never went back to Walker's house. In all the uncertainty that followed the trial and our awkward reunion, that was one thing we were both sure of. We rented a town house in the Grove, far enough from the beach so as not to stir up memories, but close enough to stay in the same school district. I figured everyone would know about me, no matter where I went, so I might as well go where I had some friends.

Some woman from a battered-women's advocacy group helped my mother find a job at a law firm. Her boss has been in trial the past few weeks, so she's been going in early and staying late. I haven't seen much of her lately. It's okay. Things are still awkward between us. I don't know whether I've forgiven her for being weak. I do know I want to be stronger.

When she sees me, she smiles. "You're up early."

"Roster's today." I pour myself a bowl of Smart Start with milk, slopping some of it onto the counter.

"Don't forget to clean that up," she says.

"In a minute." I slide the bowl onto the table across from her.

"Well, good luck today," she says.

"I don't believe in luck," I say.

"Neither do I, actually. But I hope you get what you deserve."

I hear the apology in her voice. I hear it a lot. Since my mother got out of jail, our lives have been spent pretty much in counseling. Individual counseling, family counseling, battered-women's support group—

all to tell us it wasn't our fault, like Kirstie said. I'm trying to believe that, and I *say* I do. I'm not sure Mom believes it yet either. It's like I told Angela. I didn't think I'd be able to forget. But now I wonder if maybe I don't need to forget. Maybe everyone you meet— people at school, people you wouldn't suspect—has something in the back of their lives, something bad they don't talk about and just know is there. Maybe we're all like the carnies, but maybe we don't all run. Maybe some people stay there and deal with it. Like Karpe did. And Angela. I like to think that's true, because then I could deal with it too.

I finish my cereal and see my mother sponging up the mess on the counter.

"I said I'd do it," I say.

"I don't mind. I like it neat."

I make sure to rinse out the bowl and put it in the dishwasher before I head to school.

I went to see Kirstie last summer, in Louisiana. I met her sister, Erica, who I was picturing as a little kid, but who's really about my age, and also this guy named Casey, who Kirstie met at night school. She said he wasn't her boyfriend, but I got the idea he wouldn't have minded being. It was good seeing her, seeing she was okay. But it was different than at the fair. Not as real, somehow. We kept in touch by e-mail for a few months after that. But last time, the Mailer Daemon sent my e-mail back, addressee unknown.

I haven't heard from her since, but I think about her sometimes. And I dream about her. In the dream she's always like she was that first day at the fair. I think that's how I'll always see her. I like to think of her that way, in her green T-shirt, someplace where it's always sunny— a beautiful part of the past.

• • •

I'm in front of Coach's office now. It's swarming with guys from the team and guys who hope to make the team. They're the younger players, the ones who used to look up to me, and a couple who I know think it isn't fair they have to compete with someone a year older. All around, they're high-fiving, slapping backs, and generally getting more up close and personal than guys usually get. I see one skinny freshman walking away, trying not to cry. A couple of guys try to talk to me, but I push through. In a minute I know I'll be part of that whooping, back-patting mob, but somehow, it's important for me to see the roster for myself, rather than get the information secondhand.

I finally make it to the front. I look at the yellow lined legal paper and grin.

"Did you make it?" one of the sophomores asks behind me.

"Yeah," I say. "Yeah, I made it."

From Alex Flinn's latest novel *Fade to Black*

Pinedale Senior High School
"Home of the Panthers"
PINEDALE, FLORIDA

TO: Eugene Runnels, Principal
FROM: Celia Velez, Assistant
DATE: October 27
RE: Incident Involving HIV-positive Student

Alejandro Crusan, a junior, was apparently attacked this morning at the corner of East Main and Salem Court. According to his parents, Alex was en route to Dunkin' Donuts at 35 East Main at approximately 6:00 a.m. A witness, Daria Bickell, a special education (Down Syndrome) student at Pinedale, saw Alex's red SUV stopped at a red light. An assailant, said to be wearing a blue Pinedale Panthers letter jacket and carrying a baseball bat, attacked Alex's car, smashing the front windshield and passenger-side windows. When the assailant attempted to run around to the driver's side, Alex was able to drive away. The witness saw Pinedale student Clinton Cole, 16, leaving the scene.

Although this incident did not take place on school property, I have contacted the school board, and they have pledged full cooperation with local police. Due to the nature of the incident, and also Alex's HIV-positive status, police will investigate the incident under the Florida Hate Crimes statute.

CLINTON

How do they know I did it?

They ought to give me a stinking medal. If you asked most people around here "off the record," they'd agree with what I did. I mean, sure everybody wants to be politically correct—whatever that's supposed to mean. Just because Pinedale's a cow town doesn't mean we're all rednecks without opposable thumbs, no matter what people from Miami might think. But people move here because it's a safe place. Or it was. No one wants to die. All the political correctness in the world's not worth that.

And most people would agree with that, "off the record."

But on the record, there's this little problem: they can't. That's why my butt's here in a green plastic chair in Principal Runnels's office instead of a plain old wooden chair in English class where it belongs.

I've been here an hour now, since they called me out of third period. And Runny-nose is nowhere to be found. His secretary, Miss Velez, acts like he's out on some kind of top-secret school business. But I know better. The one time, I got caught with Brett and Mo in that now-notorious mascot-swiping incident—he was late then, too. When he finally showed up, he was carting groceries—eggs and milk and Chips Ahoy. You'd think a big important principal would get his wife to do the shopping. But you'd be wrong. The man is PW, and if you don't know what that means, check with me sometime when I'm in a better mood and I'll tell you.

Miss Velez walks by, trying to look casual. But I'm pretty sure she's checking to make sure I haven't bolted. I stand when she comes in the room (my daddy taught me right) and say in my politest voice, "Excuse me, Ms. Velez?" She wants to be called *Ms.*

"Yes, Clinton?"

"Um, I was thinking if Principal Runnels won't be here for a while, could I maybe go back to class? We've got a test in English, and I sure do hate to miss it."

Or, more important, I hate to miss Alyssa Black. She has that class with me. Other girls, if they're pretty, I get tongue-tied. But Alyssa's different in the way she looks at me. It's not just that she's got beautiful eyes. But she sees me different, I feel like. Other girls see a big jock who runs with the pack. With Alyssa, it's like she . . . I don't know, understands me, maybe. Is that corny? It's like she can see inside to the part that's still this little fat kid no one likes much, the part I try to hide from most people. Today's the day I was planning on asking her to homecoming. It'll put a big dent in my plans if she knows I'm in here or if I get detention. Alyssa doesn't hang with delinquents.

Miss Velez glances at the clock. When she looks back, her face is sort of hard.

"No, Clinton, you can't go to class. They'll be with you in a few minutes."

She's gone before I get the chance to ask who "they" are.

Figures she'd be against me. Alex—the guy this is all about—he's a spic like she is. Or *Latino* as my mother would say. My father says those kinds of people always stick together. "That's the problem with 'em," he'd say. "With the whole damn State of Florida, really. You work a job your whole life, then some spic fires you and hires his second cousin. It started down in Miami, but darned if it isn't spreading up north. And soon, it'll be the last American in Florida, heading out and taking the flag with him."

My father ought to know because that's what happened to him. The getting fired part. My father was one of the most powerful men in Pinedale. But when he lost his job, my mother left him. She said it was because she couldn't stand being around his "attitudes"—whatever that means—but Dad says different. He got a new job out of state, and now I hardly see him. Mom won't let me call him much either, on account of the cost of long distance and all the child support Dad *isn't* paying. Dad can't really afford to call us, either. Mom would say that's a good thing. But I miss him.

My mom and I don't see eye to eye on much. She's sort of liberal, which is really what started this whole problem with the Crusans. She's always worrying about people's rights and so forth. When my little sister, Melody, started playing with Carolina Crusan at school, Mom said fine. Then Carolina invited Melody to sleep over their house. Mom said fine again. Go. Never mind that her HIV brother's going to unleash the black plague on Pinedale, Florida. Never mind that we don't know what type of germs and spores and junk is flying around their house (I always try not to breathe too much when I'm in class with him). Just go. Have fun. I tried to tell Melody not to eat anything over there and to wash her hands and not touch any sharp objects and not drink out of the glasses (was that really unreasonable?). But Mom made me shut up. "Stop scaring her, Clinton. She might say something to the Crusans." Like she's more worried about their feelings than her own daughter's safety.

That's when I realized I needed to take matters into my own hands. With Dad gone and Mom acting sort of crazy, what choice did I have? But I wasn't going to hurt the guy or nothing. I just wanted to scare him so he'd go back where he came from before anyone got hurt. I only wanted to protect my family, like my father would've.

Mom thinks I should feel sorry for Crusan, on account of he's got AIDS. Maybe I would feel bad for him if he was living in some other town where it didn't affect me or my family, or even if he just stayed home. Or even if he didn't sit by me in two classes, for that matter, and act like *we're* a bunch of hicks. I thought about asking Mom to take us out of Pinedale. Some kids' parents did that. They let them study at home. But Mom would've said no way. She's like that. Dad would've been different. Dad would've understood.

Miss Velez shows up again. She's smiling this time, so I guess Runny-nose must've finished buying the toilet paper and made it to work. She turns back to the door.

"Right this way, gentlemen."

I look back and see it's not Runnels following her.

Hey, what are the cops doing here?

Monday, 10:50 a.m., hallway during passing period,
Pinedale High School

DARIA

> *Maybe*
> *I am*
> *a ghost*
> *people look through*
> *like water.*
>
> *Maybe*
> *I*
> *am invisible*
> *so they do not*
> *know I watch.*
>
> *Maybe they*
> *think words*
> *are invisible*
> *so I cannot*
> *hear*
> *retard, retard, retard.*
>
> *But words are not*
> *invisible.*

Me either.
And I always,
always
watch.

ALEX

My mother's crying. I make out shapes . . . IV pole, television set, window. Hospital window with flowers on the windowsill. I shut my eyes quick. Mom can't know I'm awake. My face aches a little, and the rest of me feels like it's still asleep. Like, numb. Even closing my eyes hurts, but I keep them shut tight anyway. I'm not ready to talk to anyone and, what's more, I'm not sure I can. I can't even believe this has happened, so how can I talk about it?

And my mother's crying. Again.

Last year, when I was first diagnosed with HIV, my mother cried a lot. When she finally stopped crying, my parents took me to Disney World. It was pretty cool. Even though we lived in Miami, we hadn't been in years because my sister, Carolina—who's nine, now, eight years younger than I am—had been too young to go on many rides before that. I didn't think about why we went, that I was like one of those Make-A-Wish foundation kids who wants to see Mickey before he dies. It hadn't totally sunk in yet, you know?

Even though I felt fine, Mom made me ride in this wheelchair we rented. In a stroke of brain dead-itude, I went along with it. There were tons of gimpy kids there, and we got to go right to the front at every ride. The line for Space Mountain was, like, two hours, but we shot up front and I stepped out of my wheelchair and got on. When the Disney guy let us ahead of this one family that was waiting, the dad turned to his son and said, "Don't you hate people like that—rent a wheelchair just to go first."

Mom started crying then, too. She yelled at the guy, "You should thank God you have healthy children. My son has HIV. He's dying." And all around, people who'd been happy and smiling started looking afraid or away. It ruined the whole trip.

That was the first time it really sank in that I was going to die. Me. Die.

Die.

We haven't gone back to Disney since then and, if I did, I wouldn't ride in a stinking wheelchair. I don't need one. I'm no poster boy, and I am nowhere near needing to see Mickey. Besides, they're making some big gains in AIDS medications. I could live twenty years, maybe. Maybe longer.

Or maybe not.

I don't have AIDS yet, anyway—that's the first thing anyone needs to know about me. I read all these books about it, and I know all about T-cell counts and viral loads, but the bottom line is: I was diagnosed with HIV a year ago, and I still feel fine. I'm not on meds yet. I'm hanging in, living with it. My doctors say if I keep doing what I'm supposed to, maybe they'll find a cure before I even get really sick.

So this year we didn't go to Disney. In August, before we moved here to Podunkville, Florida, we went to New York City, and my mom and Aunt Maria took me to see this Broadway play called *Rent*. It won a lot of awards, and it's about people with AIDS. Of course, of all the musicals in New York, we had to see the one about AIDS. The people in the play, they're all junkies and homosexuals, and they're dealing with the fact that they're going to die, like, tomorrow. Aunt Maria hated the show because 1) It had loud music with electric guitars and stuff, which interfered with her sleeping; 2) It was depressing; 3) She said, "None of these people are like you, Alejandro. You are an innocent victim." I guess she meant because the people in the show were in what you'd call high-risk categories. Still, I think everyone with AIDS is an innocent victim. Most of the people I've met with HIV *are* in those higher-risk categories, and who cares? I don't think anyone deserves to get sick or die. I mean, I wouldn't wish this disease on Clinton Cole, much less some innocent homosexual.

Clinton Cole is what DC Comics would call my nemesis. He's Joker to my Batman, Green Goblin to my Spidey. Since we moved to Pinedale, people have pretty much been assholes. But Clinton's, like, the uber-asshole.

The first weeks of school, it seemed like any time I turned a corner, everyone dove together, whispering. Did they think that because they were whispering, I didn't know they were talking about me? And the people who don't whisper walk right past you in the hall, looking down, pretending not to see you. I try not to get mad at those people, because I remember I used to do it myself before. When you see someone in a wheelchair or missing a leg or something, you don't want to seem like you're staring, so you look away. Which I now know is worse. And a lot of people backed up close to the wall when I walked by. The up side (if you'd call it that) was, I didn't have any trouble getting through the halls because no one would touch me.

But then there were the people like Clinton. People who didn't care what I heard or thought. When I walked into the cafeteria the second day, he stood up and said, "Go back where you came from, fag." And you could tell everyone was with him. Since then he's been doing all kinds of other crap. He wore a surgical mask one day to Government because we sit next to each other. I think he's one of the people who left threatening notes in my locker, though I don't know for sure.

We moved here for Dad's job. We'd lived in Miami all my life, and it wasn't perfect, but it was better. I had some friends, like Austin and Danny, and other guys I hung with at school. Sure, a few people were weird, but not as many. And even though I stopped playing baseball when I got diagnosed, I was on the debate team. I made it to State with my original oratory last year, and I was going to try again this year.

Then Dad's company wanted to start an office here in Pinedale (Why here? Hell if I know), and they transferred him. I knew my parents didn't want to live here in the sticks, where there isn't so much as a Target, much less a mall. We have to drive to Gainesville to find a doctor who knows how to deal with me, and there are for sure no AIDS centers here. Without me, my parents probably wouldn't have come here. They'd have choices. Dad could get a different job. But Dad had to stay with the company to keep his health insurance. We're pretty much uninsurable as new patients because of me.

And you know what the debate team at Pinedale is? Two guys who gave me the evil eye when I walked through the door. I walked right back out. It's not even worth trying to make friends in Pinedale.

And now I'm here in the hospital, listening to my mother crying because one of these rednecks thought I wasn't dying quick enough and tried to take me out early. But he didn't finish it off, so I'm here.

I hear my mother moving around, and I keep my eyes closed, so she won't know I'm awake. I can't deal with any more crying right now.

But when I close my eyes, it's like I'm there again. This morning. The sun streaming through my windshield. The baseball bat, the broken glass. The outline of some guy—the guy who attacked me.

And now I'm here, face aching, and the rest of me just numb. Numb.

Also by Alex Flinn

Hc 0-06-029198-2
Pb 0-06-447257-4

Pb 0-06-447371-6

Breathing Underwater

Intelligent, popular, handsome, and wealthy, sixteen-year-old Nick Andreas is pretty much perfect—on the outside. But no one knows the terror that Nick faces every time he is alone with his father.

Breaking Point

Paul is new to Gate, a school whose rich students make life miserable for anyone not like them. And Paul is definitely not like them. How far will he go to be one of the gang?

www.harperteen.com　　HarperTempest　　www.alexflinn.com
An Imprint of HarperCollinsPublishers